Stampede

BOOKS BY
STEWART EDWARD WHITE

FICTION
The Glory Hole

Of the Far West:
The Claim Jumpers—Blazed Trail Stories—The Westerners
The Killer—Arizona Nights—The Long Rifle

Of the Far North:
Conjuror's House—The Silent Places—Skookum Chuck
Secret Harbour—Pole Star (with Harry DeVighne)
Wild Geese Calling

Of the Lumber Woods:
The Blazed Trail—The Riverman—Blazed Trail Stories
The Rules of the Game

Of California:
Stampede—The Rules of the Game—The Gray Dawn
Gold—The Rose Dawn—On Tiptoe
Ranchero—Folded Hills—Old California

Of Mystery:
The Mystery (with Samuel Hopkins Adams)
The Sign at Six

Of Africa:
The Leopard Woman—Simba—Back of Beyond

ADVENTURE
The Out of Doors—Exploration
The Forest—Camp and Trail—The Mountains
The Land of Footprints—The Cabin
African Campfires—The Pass—The Rediscovered
Country—Lions in the Path

HISTORICAL AND PHILOSOPHICAL
Old California: In Pictures and Story
The 'Forty-niners—Daniel Boone: Wilderness Scout
Credo—Why Be a Mud Turtle?
Dog Days—The Betty Book—Across the Unknown
(With Harwood White)
The Unobstructed Universe

JUVENILE
The Magic Forest
The Adventures of Bobby Orde

Stampede

STEWART EDWARD WHITE

DOUBLEDAY, DORAN AND COMPANY, INC.
Garden City, New York
1942

PRINTED AT THE *Country Life Press*, GARDEN CITY, N. Y., U. S. A.

CL

COPYRIGHT, 1935, 1942
BY STEWART EDWARD WHITE
ALL RIGHTS RESERVED

FIRST EDITION

Stampede

I

A FAT and rather untidy man sat in a boxlike office in the second story of a building near Portsmouth Square. In those days that was not far from the water front, and the man could look directly out to the Bay where lay, rotting at their chains, scores of wooden vessels, deserted by their crews for the gold rush of '49, and since superseded by the faster clippers made necessary by the shifts of trade. He sprawled back in his chair, his booted feet on the flat desk, his black wide hat over his eyes. In his mouth was an unlighted cigar which he revolved methodically with his teeth and tongue. The end of the cigar had become frayed in the process. Every so often the man removed it momentarily to blow forth at random small wet pieces of tobacco that had become detached.

He was alone in the room, which was small and ostentatiously plain both in ornament and furnishing: a pine box, carpeted with coco matting; a few shelves of lawbooks; another, less comfortable, chair; and a spittoon. This crudeness was unnecessary, a pose; for San Francisco was some years out of its swaddling clothes, and Jake Conger's fortune by now was tidily on toward the seven figures.

Jake continued to stare at the abandoned ships. After a time, absent-mindedly, he struck a match and applied the flame to the end of the cigar. Only with some difficulty, and considerable mechanical ingenuity, did he manage to get the poor demoralized thing going. He persisted patiently, though a half-dozen fresh cheroots peeped from his vest pocket.

Behind him the door opened and closed.

"Hullo?" said Jake Conger inquiringly, but without bothering to turn his head.

"Jake!" cried an amused voice on a note of false alarm, "your chewing tobacco's on fire!"

The fat man withdrew his booted feet from the desk top, swiveled about to face his visitor. The latter was as slender as the other was fat; as spick and span as the other was untidy; a man perhaps rising fifty, but with the fresh skin and snapping live eyes of youth. He was dressed in the height of one of the half-score of fashions affected by the San Francisco of that day: a high flaring collar above a wide bow stock; a low-cut waistcoat; an ample blue coat with a wide rolled collar and tails behind; tight-fitting striped pantaloons strapped beneath the insteps of varnished boots. In one hand he skillfully carried a polished cane, a pair of gloves, and a tall hat. A roach of upstanding white hair alone gave him his proper age.

Jake Conger's shrewd eyes half closed, but he showed no other indication of surprise. With one foot he dextrously spun the vacant chair toward his visitor, and at the same time, as though with the same motion, he produced more cigars, but from an inside pocket.

"Set! Smoke!" he invited curtly.

The newcomer spread his tails, seated himself, laid aside his hat and stick.

"Yours, or political?" he inquired, examining the cigars.

"Mine," said Conger. He touched his outside pocket.

"Political," he added, "next my heart, always, Braidwood."

"In that case——" accepted the visitor. He puffed for a moment until the cheroot was well alight. "You seemed busy when I came in."

"I was looking at them ships," said the fat man with sudden and surprising animation, as though he had just awakened, "and figgering. Seems like they ought to be good for *something*. A man could get 'em cheap: for nothing, practically."

"You might pass a law," suggested the visitor blandly, "turn 'em into prison ships, like the old *Euphemia*. You'll have enough jailbirds to fill 'em all if things go on as they are. But look here, Jake, I didn't come in to waste your time. I want you to do me a favor."

"I thought likely," grunted Conger, but not unamiably. "Let's hear it."

"I want a job."

"A job!" repeated Jake, after an instant of blank incredulity. "F'r you? A job? What are you talking about?"

"Not for me," laughed Braidwood, "for someone else. And it has to be an especial sort of job. That's why I came to you. There's nothing in it—for anybody," he added at Conger's expression, then laughed. "I'll tell you about it," he suggested.

"So do," grumbled Conger. The cigar began again its methodical revolution, the movement imperiling the integrity of the ash, which had grown to an inch or more in length. "Permit me," said Braidwood. He whisked an ash tray from the desk, held it beneath the end of the cheroot which he delicately flicked with the nail of his little finger. Conger grunted. "Do not mention it," said the visitor.

2

"It is for my nephew," Braidwood began his explanation.

"Didn't know you had one," growled Conger.

"He has been here but a little over a week. He arrived on the clipper *Thunder Bird*. I wish to find him suitable occupation."

"Why don't you give him a job yourself?" growled Conger. "You ought to have any amount of them."

"I could; here. But he is pretty young—just twenty—and——"

"No good, eh?" interrupted Conger. "So it's to be a government job! Well," he admitted cynically, "don't know but you're right."

"He's a fine boy," Braidwood denied heatedly, "and he's going to make a fine and able man, but——"

"But what?" Jake Conger grinned.

"But he's young; that's all: he's just *young*, and this town is bad for him, at least till he gets his feet under him."

"Twenty's not so young," said Conger. "Why, I mind me when I——"

"It isn't years; it's age—or rather it's youth, just sheer youth. Some grow up quicker than others."

"Say"—Jake leaned forward so suddenly that even his heavy chair protested—"that wasn't your nephew by any chance that I heerd 'em tellin' of that got into a row with Yankee Sullivan at the El Dorado a night or so ago?"

Braidwood nodded. Conger removed the wreck of the cigar from his mouth in order to whistle. "Suicidal tendencies, eh?" he remarked dryly.

"Claimed he saw Sullivan slip a card on a *Chileño*," said Braidwood.

"So he had to horn in! How did he figger in it, even if 'twas so? And what if it was? Who cares about a *Chileño*, anyways?"

"I know, I know!" agreed Braidwood with a slight

show of impatience. "But that's just the point. He's young and he's green and he's enthusiastic and he's come out West just honing for what he calls adventure. You know yourself, Jake, that that is a bad combination the way this town is put together right now. If it hadn't been for Danny Randall and Diamond Jack, Yankee Sullivan would have killed him the other night."

"Sure! I heard about that!" Conger contemplated the debris of the cigar with regret, finally cast it accurately into the spittoon. "Well, what is it you want of me?"

"I told you. A job for him. Something away from the city, with some responsibility to it—or at least something that looks responsible. Leslie is nobody's fool."

"Ain't many jobs with dry nurses to 'em," said Conger dryly.

Braidwood frowned.

"Now don't get me wrong, Conger," he said sharply. "The lad is nobody's fool, and he can take care of himself and he'll learn fast. But he's very young and he's idealistic——"

"Oh, I see your p'int," the fat man interrupted. He thoughtfully produced another cheroot and stuck it in his mouth. Braidwood watched him.

"He is the son of my youngest sister," said Braidwood

after a little. "I have not seen her since she was a baby, five or six years old. That's a long time. But I was very fond of her, and she must have been very fond of me and talked of me. At any rate, when she died the boy came straight out here to me. Of course it may have been merely a spirit of adventure—the West, the gold fields. I don't know." He was talking more to himself than to Conger.

"Well, I tell you: I got a kind of idea," said the latter thickly over the obstruction of the cheroot.

"You know the gov'ment is tackling the land business lately, examining titles and adjusting boundaries and the like." He waved his hand toward the papers that strewed the top of the desk. "Big job. All mixed up." He chuckled fatly. "Good pickings. Well, I think I could get this boy of yours an appointment as Field Inspector. How'd that be?"

"I don't know. What is it? What does it amount to?"

"Nothing much. Just takes the grants and plots and checks up on landmarks and boundaries, and so on, and makes a report as to whether everything gees or not."

"And if it doesn't?"

"Well, then mebbe the land is declared public and open for entry, or maybe suit is entered in Federal

Courts. It all depends." Conger grinned reminiscently. "I should say it did depend! You'd better send your boy into a den of grizzly b'ars as up the Valley where the squatters are strong. They make their own land laws and they don't want no interference—unless it interferes their way. But I was thinking we could send him up past Soledad. There's a lot of *ranchos* up there, so far back that nobody even knows they're there. How's it strike you?"

Braidwood nodded.

"I knew I could depend on you, Jake. I won't forget it."

"I don't intend you shall," returned Conger dryly. "That's all right. Send him around to see me."

II

LESLIE DAYTON said good-by to his uncle and clambered aboard the stage for San Jose. He had no regrets at leaving the excitements of San Francisco, for he was of the forward-looking type that peers always over the horizon. There true adventure ever dwells, though to the impartial observer it would seem that enough of that commodity could be picked up in any street or alley of the young city. Indeed Leslie had thought such to be the case and had plunged into the excitements of the place with an eager and reckless zest that completely submerged his first slight disappointment that he was not at once to go gold hunting in the placers. Braidwood laughed indulgently at this idea.

"You're three years too late," said he. "That's all over—I mean the romance. Oh, there's gold yet, but it's down mostly to plain hard work. The fortunes are being made right here."

The boy had snapped eagerly at the position offered him by the lawyer-politician as soon as he learned that it was to take him into what, to him, was also a dwelling place of romance—the ranch country of the old regime. To Conger's surprise, and somewhat to his amusement, young Dayton proved to be not only quick of mental grasp, but deadly earnest in his efforts to prepare himself.

"You're right," he told Braidwood, "he's quite a youngster. And he's going to make quite a man—if he lives that long. I told him I wanted him to pull out right away, and he talked an arm off me, insisting he couldn't possibly get ready inside a week. I gave in to save my ears." Conger chuckled. "He's going to let me know when he's ready to go," he added dryly.

"A week!" echoed Braidwood, aghast. "But that won't do."

"If you're thinking of Yankee Sullivan," said Jake Conger comfortably, "rest yore mind. I've spoke my word, and he'll behave, and so will all that gang as long as they know the kid is gittin' out soon. I wouldn't answer if he was staying on. And I don't reckon you need worry about his getting into no more trouble, either."

"I wish I had your confidence." Braidwood shook his head.

"He's going to be too busy."

"Busy! At what?"

"Gitting him a good ready." The fat man dropped his chair to its four legs and leaned his elbows on the desk. "You know where he is now?"

"I'm getting afraid to guess where he is at any time."

"Well, he's at Judge McCain's law library. That kid's going to know more land law than I know myself before he gets through. I tried to tell him 'twa'n't necessary, that all he had to do was report back what he saw and we'd tend to the law part of it, but he said, if it was all the same to me, he'd ruther know what he was doing."

"Well!" ejaculated Braidwood, impressed. He ran his hand through his upstanding white hair, shook his head. "You surprise me! I never would have suspected him of anything like thoroughness—or interest, for that matter."

"I'll let you know when he gives me my orders." And Jake chuckled again with vast relish.

Stampede

Nevertheless the week had still two days to go when Jake was recalled from his favorite occupation of staring across the Bay by a knock at his door. So unusual a phenomenon was this that he removed his feet and slewed his chair about before answering.

"Come in!" he shouted.

The door opened and closed.

"Oh, it's you!" said Jake Conger. He surveyed the visitor for some moments speculatively, with an approval that was completely cynical, somewhat reluctant, but still was approval. This was a compact, medium-sized young man, wiry rather than muscular. He was as dark of complexion as some Spaniards, with good-looking regular features of no peculiar distinction; characteristics he probably shared in general with a half hundred other youngsters in this community of young men. But even in Jake Conger's eyes he stood out as both individual and arresting. This was due to two things, or rather to two different manifestations of the same thing. His eyes, and to a lesser degree the set of his mouth, expressed an outgoing eagerness: from his whole being emanated a vibrant vitality which reminded Jake Conger of nothing so much as his setter dog, Shot, awaiting his command to move forward. The young man had stopped just inside the door. He held his hat in his two hands and fixed his brilliant eyes on the lawyer, waiting for him to speak.

"Well?" said the latter after a moment.

"I'm all ready," announced the boy. Beneath the studied evenness of his voice was a lilt of eagerness.

"Know what you're to do, eh? And how to do it?"

"Yes, sir."

"More'n I do," said Conger dryly, but he said it to himself. "You got your maps of that country, and you copied out those records like I told you?"

"Yes, sir; all finished."

"Well then, come here." The fat man opened a drawer of his desk from which he drew a document ornamented with a red seal. He contemplated it a moment, then thrust it negligently across the desk. "Thar's your commission," said he. "Hold up your right hand. You do solemnly swear that you will"—he gabbled rapidly through a form of oath, the words tumbling and slurring—"s' help you God?" he ended and looked up. Something in the boy's eyes dragged him to his feet.

"So help me God," repeated Leslie Dayton under his breath. "I do," he said aloud. He took the paper almost reverently, looked at it a moment.

"That's all," said Jake, recovering himself and flopping down again into his chair. "When do you start?"

"Tomorrow." The boy hesitated. "Don't I wear a shield, or a star, or something like that?"

Conger suppressed a grin.

"No, son," said he. "Them things go with sheriffs and marshals. That dockyment is your authority. Take care of it. Remember now," he added with faint irony, "you're a responsible officer of the United States gov'nment. Good-by and good luck."

"Good-by, sir." The young man shifted uneasily, finally blurted out: "I want to tell you, sir, how deeply I appreciate this chance and how grateful I am to you. I haven't much experience, but I'm going to do the best I can to keep you from regretting your trust in me."

Jake Conger, to his profound surprise and somewhat to his anger, felt his face flush.

"All right! All right!" he growled. "Good-by. Let me hear from you."

2

It had been decided, as most expedient, that Leslie should go by the regular stagecoaches to San Jose, then to San Juan Bautista. At the latter place he must buy a suitable horse through the offices of a man to whom he would be accredited; after which he would proceed in due course over the mountains to the valley of the Salinas, and so to the scene of his proposed investigations. For this purpose Braidwood supplied him with a small sum of money, which he carried next to his skin in a soft leather belt with pockets, but more liberally with letters of recommendation to various people, like the man at San Juan, with whom Braidwood's wide business interests had relation. These letters, together with the commission with the red seal and maps and papers, Leslie carried wrapped in oiled silk in a pair of aggressively new saddlebags along with a change of clothing. This made rather a clumsy and heavy parcel. Braidwood tentatively suggested so and pointed out that a pack horse would make possible a less meager equipment, but desisted instantly he perceived that the boy saw this expedition as a kind of lone sortie, on his own resources, into a wilderness. That was part of the excitement and went with the little two-barreled derringer and the huge Colt's revolving pistol that Leslie brought home from his first shopping. Braidwood looked on these more than doubtfully.

"Those things are just likely to make trouble for you,"

he objected. "I've never carried a pistol, and I've never had difficulty, even when things were pretty rough; before we squelched the Hounds. If you're known to be unarmed, they're likely to leave you alone." However, he did not press the point. He refrained carefully from issuing too much advice or warning. Leslie must cut his teeth on life in his own way. So he clambered aboard the stage with the two-barreled derringer up his sleeve, the way Danny Randall carried it, the Colt's revolving pistol strapped about his waist, the overstuffed saddlebags at his feet.

The stage was a high, open affair with five seats, each capable of accommodating three. That occupied by the driver, of course, faced forward. The remaining four faced one the other, in pairs. This day there were, including Leslie, only a half-dozen passengers. One, on invitation, sat with the driver. This was a young man, tall and well knit, who climbed to his place with a swing of grace that attested great power in control. He wore a long linen duster, well buttoned, and a flat, low-crowned Spanish hat. The darkness of his complexion and hair and the handsome regularity of his features might, indeed, have indicated a Spanish origin, but his eyes were of the uncompromising steel gray found in none but the northern races. The expression of his countenance was grave and self-contained. His glance crossed Leslie's briefly, without expression. Nevertheless Leslie felt somehow appraised and young, though he realized resentfully that this youth's years were no more than his own. He flushed and climbed to his own place. For the moment he rather regretted having buckled on the Colt's revolving pistol quite so prominently. But the next passenger was similarly armed, so he felt better.

This man was a rough-looking customer, long and angular, his lean, sallow face covered with stubble of a length that left one in doubt as to whether he was merely unshaven or was starting a beard. His eyes were heavy-lidded, but here again one must remain in doubt whether this expression was of insolence or a physical characteristic. He wore rough garments, a queer mixture of frontier and city, the trousers tucked in fancy-stitched boots, and with it a scattering of Spanish ornamentation—silver *conchas* studding belt and holster, a plaited horsehair band to his hat, soft leather cuffs to his shirt. Leslie could not make him out. He looked formidable. He settled himself in the seat opposite, spat copiously overside, looked the boy over from head to foot.

Two other travelers, in no way remarkable, took places

in the seats back of Leslie. At the last moment, as the driver gathered his reins, a small rotund man appeared, climbed nimbly up the two iron steps, and plumped down opposite Leslie. He was slightly out of breath, but he smiled inclusively and uttered a greeting. At first glance he seemed a simple friendly soul, for his face was round, his clear china-blue eyes as round as his face, and set so wide apart that his whole expression was of radiating candor. He wore a folded linen coat.

Hardly had he seated himself when the hostlers at the leaders' heads sprang aside; the driver released the brake with a thrust of his foot; the long-lashed whip cracked like a pistol.

The route led out of town by way of the Mission Dolores, over a plank road on which the horses' hoofs clattered resoundingly. This was a new part of town to Leslie, and he hung out the side of the stage. Beyond the mission were two race tracks and a bull ring, and as this was a holiday, the plank road was acrowd with interest. The stage plowed through regardless, scattering the pedestrians and horsemen right and left, forcing the other wheeled vehicles perilously near the edge of the planking, beyond which was deep sand or mud and almost the certainty of an overturn. Nevertheless, no one seemed to take this in bad part. They scrambled hastily out of the way, but once in safety they waved their hats at the stage and grinned and shouted after it. The driver, the numerous reins held delicately high, the whip slanted across, looked straight ahead, paying them no attention. It was as if, to him, the road was empty. The stage rolled grandly in the hollow reverberations from the planks, and unconsciously Leslie partook of its immense superiority, and himself became a superior being looking down from the immunities of privilege.

Then suddenly the ear-filling roar of the wheels ceased, so abruptly that it was like the casting aside of a garment. The stage moved more quietly, less swiftly, over the soft earth of the county road. And to it solitude had come as swiftly as quiet, for the rabble of miners, hoodlums, Chinese and Mexicans afoot, the stream of buggies, carts, coaches, and the elegant calèches of the beautiful ladies had turned off at right angles to the race tracks and the bull ring. The occasion was off parade. The horses moderated their pace to a purposeful swift trot. The driver flipped deftly the long trailing lash of his whip into a loop about its stock and thrust it in its socket. He turned to talk to his neighbor. The passengers sat back relaxed. The landscape, which had been thrust aside for smaller pomposities, moved in close to take its rightful preponderance, so that the misty Visitación hills and the sleepily glinting wide waters of the Bay and the blue distances of the Contra Costa shores reasserted their quietude, across which the tiny stagecoach crawled in a proper insignificance.

This was all new and strange to Leslie, immensely exciting. There was nothing like any of it in his former Pennsylvania home. Except perhaps the meadowlarks that perched atop things and sang golden liquid notes. They looked the same, but the things they sang were different. Leslie's eyes roved avidly the wayside, eager for each fresh surprise. And the surprises were many—a movement of plumed quail over the gracious shoulder of a hill, hundreds of them, thousands of them, so that it was as though the whole ground shifted; an immense rabbit with ears that seemed to Leslie as long as a mule's; wild fowl rising suddenly from a little near-by pond which their close-packed bodies had obscured so that Leslie had not suspected any pond at all, and the whistling of their wings like the keening of a heavy wind; an iridescent red-and-gold jewel of a hummingbird that came straight at the stage like a bullet and poised on misty wings for several seconds not two feet from Leslie's face and was gone. The road wound in and out the flanks of the hills, each bend a disclosure and a surprise, and each rise to a crest an anticipation. And in the sky great birds circling stately, which Leslie thought might be eagles, but was not sure.

So vibrantly absorbed was he by these and many other things that he was aware of little else until a chance phrase caught him from the conversation of the two men opposite him.

"No right to the land!" the rough-looking customer was saying incredulously. "Haven't we taken the country?"

"That fact hardly gives title over those who already owned it," suggested the other, but lazily, without conviction.

"Own it, hell! Who are they? A passel of greasers too lazy to make any use of it. What right has ary one man to own fifty thousand acres? I ask you that."

"Don't ask me." The smaller man waved a hand in disclaimer.

"Well, I'll tell you!" returned the other. "They got it by cheating and false swearing and just plain bribing. Micheltorena issued land grants after he was kicked out from being governor. Pico sold 'em fast as he could as soon as he seen the country was going to be American.

Way I look at it that all these old grants just plain lapsed when the country was took over. You mean to tell me different?" He thrust his face forward truculently. The little man seemed unalarmed.

"Not at all," he said amusedly. "But I still am inclined to speculate on what the law is going to say finally to these squatters—for that is exactly what they are. And how they expect to get title."

"Law! title!" The other spat contemptuously overside. "The boys across the Bay's got the right idea. They've took up their hundred and sixty acres apiece, like they got a right to anywhere——"

"On public land, not private land," murmured the small man.

The other paused to glare but made no direct answer.

"And they're raising crops. Danged good crops, too! I tell you, there's a heap of land in Californy, and there's a passel of folks coming across the plains looking for it. And when anyone asks them where's their title, they got a cannon, and they point to that and tell 'em there's their title, and it's good enough."

"Let's see, what's the name of the man the land belongs to—is supposed to belong to?" the small man corrected himself.

"Oh, an old greaser named Peralta. He claimed to own the whole shore and way back into the hills. We showed him better."

"We? You claim land there?"

"I sort of got the boys settled."

"Peralta; that's it. I remember. Put him in jail, didn't you, and fined him—for attempting to put off trespassers —what he called trespassers, that is? Isn't that pretty rough?"

"I'd like to know why. He's got to be l'arned. Don't waste no tears on that old son of a bitch. He'd steal you blind. He's a greaser, I tell you, and I never seen one yet that wasn't a dirty liar and a thief."

The young man on the front seat turned his head, gravely surveyed the speaker for a moment, and turned back again.

The stage rounded the last of Visitación's shoulders and came out upon a wide plain between the Santa Cruz mountains and the Bay. Here were spaced live oaks and ripening grasses that bent in the breeze, and bands of cattle here and there, and watercourses with sycamores voiced with the soft mourning of doves. The coolness of the upper end of the peninsula gave way to the power of the sun, so that the dust of the road awakened from its damp sleep and enveloped the vehicle in a cloud. The stage driver and the other passengers produced wide bandannas of cotton or silk, which they tied loosely across the lower parts of their faces. The small man buttoned his long linen coat to his chin. Leslie, inexperienced in this sort of travel, had provided no such protection. The dust was powder fine. The slightest wind current lifted it. A ground squirrel, scampering across, raised a cloud of it that hung in the air and resettled slowly and reluctantly.

"I suppose," the bigger man continued the conversation in muffled tones, "that you figger good American citizens are agoing to pack up and git off'n their own property just because a lot of lawyers tell 'em to!"

"I wouldn't dare guess."

"Wouldn't you fight ef'n somebody tried to put you off yore farm that you'd t'iled and sweat over to make yourself a home in the wilderness?" insisted the other oratorically.

"Probably! Probably!" conceded the small man. "And," he added, "I'd probably do a little fighting if a gang of cutthroats came and sat down on land I'd always owned and declined to get off."

"Hell!" said the other man contemptuously. "That kind ain't got no fight in 'em!"

The small man burst out laughing.

"That's the spirit!" he cried. He fumbled beneath the folds of his duster and produced a silver-mounted flask. "Wet your whistle," he invited. "This is the driest dust I ever saw. Drink hearty!" he urged. "Here's hoping you find what you want."

The other accepted the flask readily enough but eyed its donor suspiciously.

"Now what do you mean by that?"

"Why, you're looking for land yourself, aren't you?" The other continued to eye him in silence. "No offense. It's nothing to me." He retrieved the flask and offered it to Leslie, who touched it to his lips. "If you find anything real good you might let me know. I might turn farmer myself. How much could you use, stranger? How many in your gang?" He turned his wide blue eyes on the other, a certain insolence beneath their blank, candid surfaces. Leslie looked from one to the other, perplexed.

Shortly the stage drew up at a tiny shack carrying a huge sign—Ten Mile House—and behind it a series of corrals with horses. Here the team was to be changed. The passengers descended to walk about, climbing a little stiffly down the series of small iron steps. The young man in the front seat with the driver, however, vaulted over the high front wheel to the ground as lightly as a cat. He turned at once to address Leslie's neighbor who had so freely aired his views. His head was back; his gray eyes were cold and level; the curves of the lower part of his handsome face had hardened.

"I have overheard what you have been saying," he said clearly and loudly. "I wish to state that Don Luis Peralta is an honorable man and a gentleman who has been most foully treated by a parcel of blackguards and cutthroats, and anyone who says different lies."

The man stared, struck motionless and speechless for a moment by sheer astonishment. The bystanders took advantage of this pause to move with considerable celerity to right and left. Leslie looked from one to the other of the principals, himself a trifle bewildered. Then slowly the man's chest heaved in a deep breath. His lips drew back.

"Are you calling me a liar?" he asked softly at length.

"You've called yourself that a dozen times," said the young man. His hands hung loosely at his sides; his eyes held the other steadily. Leslie was suddenly invaded by a panic of haste. He alone, beside these two, seemed alive. The others were like a group of wax figures, so still and impartially attentive were they. Good God, did none of them intend to interfere? Could not they see the man's hand stealing backward to his holster? Were they going to stand aside while murder was committed, murder of an unarmed man? Belatedly Leslie remembered the Colt's revolving pistol at his own belt, for the man's hand was already on the butt of his own weapon. He snatched for it and tugged at it, but it stuck in the new stiff leather; and at any rate, his swifter thoughts realized, it would be too late.

"By God!" cried someone.

The half-drawn pistol had clattered to the ground. Its owner was holding his right wrist with his left hand and staring incredulously at a knife transfixing his forearm.

Leslie managed at length to wrench his own weapon free. He rushed forward and thrust it into the young man's hand. The latter nodded without looking at him.

"Thanks," said he briefly. "There's no need."

Nevertheless he accepted the weapon.

As though his movement had released the occasion, the bystanders now crowded about.

"By God!" cried one. "That was the slickest thing I ever saw!"

"Your hand, sir! I'm free to confess I never saw faster work!"

Stampede

"He deserved what he got!" cried a third effusively.

"Like a snake, by gad! Like a snake striking!"

The young man, however, shook them off impatiently. He addressed the stage driver, who still stood apart, chewing a nonchalant quid.

"Better take a look at him, Jim," said he, "and get me back my knife."

The driver nodded and stepped forward to comply.

"I'm a doctor," spoke up the small rotund man. He took charge of the cursing victim.

"Let go your arm," he commanded. "How can I do anything?" He drew out the knife with a sudden deft motion and applied his thumbs to the lips of the wound. "Water," he commanded the stage driver, "and bring me my bag."

Most of the bystanders, including Leslie, crowded close to watch his operations. Some talked apart. No one, for the moment, approached the young man who stood leaning idly against the front wheel of the stage. The hostlers resumed the changing of the team.

The doctor worked busily and skillfully, talking the while, partly to himself, partly to his patient, partly to his assistant.

"Clean incision—skipped the artery. Hold still. Of

course it hurts; it may hurt more. You're lucky, no artery punctured, no tendons cut; good as ever soon. . . . Fresh water. . . . Anybody got a larger handkerchief? . . . If that starts to bleed through let me know. . . . Pour the rest of that over my hands." He straightened his back. He seemed abruptly to have forgotten the existence of the man he had been treating, to be unaware of the crowding spectators, so that miraculously he and the stage driver seemed to be alone together. "That was like lightning, Jim," he observed, drying his hands reflectively on a bandanna. "Like a rattlesnake. I suppose it was no lucky accident? The only man I ever heard of who was said to be able to handle a knife like that was a man named Burnett, an old-timer. They told some steep yarns of what he could do."

"Yon lad's name is Djo Burnett," said the stage driver.

The doctor looked across at the young man.

"So!" He picked up the knife and wiped it on the bandanna, which he threw away. He also possessed himself of the desperado's pistol from the dust where it had fallen. Briskly he stepped across to the youth.

"Here's your snickersnee," said he, "and you'd better take charge of this thing for a while."

"How is he?" The young man nodded his thanks. He

Stampede 31

thrust the knife into a sheath beneath the linen duster and handed the revolver to Jim.

"Clean incision. No major blood vessels cut, nor tendons. He'll be all right in a fortnight."

"That's good," said Djo Burnett.

"Could you do that again?" asked the doctor curiously.

"Why, he wasn't three yards away!" Djo appeared faintly astonished.

"Yes, I reckon you could," concluded the doctor with satisfaction. "But I don't see yet how you did it! *I* didn't see you move. How the devil could you get at the thing so fast?"

"The knife? Oh, I had that in my hand. I'd be a fool to talk trouble without being ready for trouble." He looked about at the ring of interested observers, obviously embarrassed at so much publicity. But the little doctor was like a terrier on a root. His was the scientific mind: he wanted always to get at the bottom of things.

"Why didn't you kill him?" he persisted. "You could have."

"Too much trouble." Djo was recovering his self-possession and about to take control. He turned to the stage driver. "About ready, Jim?"

"Oh yes, I see; to be sure." The doctor glanced at the

late victim, his arm in a sling, glowering in the background.

"Git aboard," summoned the driver. "We better be gitting on. Here, you," he called to the wounded man, "you git up here with me. No, I mean it. We ain't going to have any more trouble while I'm in charge. Climb up where I can keep an eye on you."

The man grunted contemptuously, but he obeyed.

"You'll hear from me again," he promised Djo; and to Leslie, "As for you, greenhorn, you better l'arn to keep out of what ain't your business."

"Come on! Climb!" said Jim, unimpressed.

3

The hero of this episode took his place alongside Leslie.

"Here's your pistol," said he, "and I want to thank you again. It's a beauty. I wish I had one like that. My father has one of the first ones that ever came out here, and he's promised me one when I can beat him shooting. That'll be never, I guess," the young man sighed.

Reassured that his wearing of the weapon was not scorned, Leslie slipped it back in its holster.

"It was nothing," he muttered. "Nobody could stand by and see a man murdered in cold blood." He laughed. "But you don't need any pistol. I never saw anything like that. Is it difficult?"

"Not that close. Just a trick. Takes practice."

"It was a mighty fine thing to do."

The other boy's face flushed slowly.

"It was foolish," he acknowledged candidly. "My father is going to give me the devil when he hears about it. He thinks it's foolish to fight unless you have to."

"But you certainly had to," cried Leslie loyally; "you'd have been killed otherwise."

His companion smiled wryly.

"I didn't have to get into the mess in the first place. What difference does it make what that sort says?" He changed the subject abruptly. "My name is Djo Burnett," said he. "You spell it D-j-o."

"I am Leslie Dayton. I am from Philadelphia. Have you been out here long?"

"Me? Oh, I was born here." Djo brushed this aside. "Philadelphia?" he cried. "And have you been to New York?"

His steady gravity had dropped from him, and with it the illusion of greater maturity and more years. He was of an age with his companion. He plied Leslie with eager questions of the great cities of the East and their peoples and their customs.

"It must be wonderful!" he sighed. "I've never seen a city. Only Monterey and this new San Francisco. But they are not the same. I'd like to go back there. I'd like to go to one of the colleges. Have you been to college?"

"Only for a year, at the Boston college of Harvard. Then my mother died, and I came out here to my uncle, her brother."

"Ah, I am sorry," said Djo gently. Then after a moment, "Is he all you have left?"

"No, no"—Leslie hastily disclaimed the pathetic role—"but—well, you see, I wanted to get out here——"

"Been to the diggings?" asked Djo shrewdly.

"My uncle says it is too late for them."

Djo nodded. "Yes, that's so, I guess. The fun's mostly out of it now. Five years ago——"

"Did you see them?"

"Oh, I was too young. I wanted to, but my father wouldn't let me."

"He went, didn't he? Did he have any luck?"

"No, he didn't go."

"I thought everybody went, according to the stories they tell."

"Almost everybody did. But you see one side of my family is Spanish. My mother is Spanish. My grandfather is a very wise man, an *hidalgo*. When they found this gold, and everybody dropped everything and began to rush to the placers, Don Sylvestro—that's my grandfather—called in all my uncles and all the family to talk it over. This is what he said to us: that God must have intended the gold for the Americans. 'If he had wanted the Spanish to have had it,' he said, 'he would have let them discover it before now. So do not go after it. Go back to the *ranchos*. Raise meat, for these people must eat while they live.'"

"So did none of you go?" asked Leslie, curious.

Djo opened his eyes in surprise.

"Why, for sure not! Don Sylvestro is the head of the family!"

Leslie remembered the enormous upheaval in his own family before he was allowed to come West.

"But your father—he is not Spanish," he pointed out.

"No, but he is of the family," replied Djo, as though this settled it.

The stage had by now left the shore of the Bay. Through the wide flat gap between the hills of Visitación and the beginnings of the Santa Cruz mountains sucked a westerly breeze, bringing with it a faint, far tang of the sea. It flattened the lazy dust clouds, bore them away in long streamers low to the ground.

"Whee, that's better!" cried Leslie, breathing deep of the unsullied air.

The passengers undid the protective bandannas and handkerchiefs, wiped their faces, beat themselves partially free from the powder of dust.

"It's no way to travel," said Djo contemptuously. "We shan't get into San Jose before dark. California fashion we'd do it in six hours."

"Sixty miles? What do you do: fly?"

Djo explained. A half-dozen horses apiece, *vaqueros* to drive them and shift saddles, frequent changes of mount before anyone tired, abandoning any that showed signs of actual exhaustion.

"Though that is not often; our horses are good," said he.

"I'd be the one to be abandoned," chuckled Leslie. "I'd never be able to ride sixty miles. I'd die."

But he got the impression of a certain magnificence that inspired his imagination. He turned the tables on Djo, began to question in his turn. Djo knew everything. He knew the smallest animals, the tiniest birds, often by only a flick of color, a flutter of wing, or a single note of song caught above the rumble and creak of the stage. He knew the reasons for apparent foolishness, such as the broad leather band, or corset, fully eight inches wide, that the stage driver wore about his middle. It was studded with silver *conchas* and embroidered in intricate patterns of stitches, and Leslie had imagined it sheer swank and display, with which, secretly, he sympathized. But it seemed the thing had sense.

"You'll know why before you get to Monterey," said Djo. "You'll feel as if your insides had been jarred loose, and you'll be so sore around the body that you can't wiggle." He showed Leslie that he had bound his own waist close with a number of folds of a broad Spanish sash. "It's no way to travel," he repeated, "but sometimes you've got to do it."

In spite of Djo's scorn, however, the stage made good time. It was part of a service new since the Occupation. Leslie had difficulty in understanding that only so few years ago wheeled vehicles were practically unknown in California—except *carretas* and a few state carriages. Djo described *carretas*. Behind his habitually grave expression was hidden a delightful humor. Leslie shouted with laughter.

Every ten miles or so they stopped briefly for a change of horses. On these occasions the passengers debarked for a hasty stretch of the leg. But not for long. Jim, the driver, herded them aboard. He permitted no unnecessary delay. The company was proud of the fact that it covered the distance to San Jose in a single day. Nevertheless it was a hard and jolting journey; and, in spite of his interest in new things and his vital youth, Leslie found himself lapsing into longer and longer silences as the day progressed. When at last the stage made its dashing entrance into the sprawling little town and drew up before the crude frame structure of its leading hotel, he was glad of the cool basin of water and the bed in the little redwood box of a room assigned to him.

There he fell promptly asleep, nor did he stir until aroused by the beating of a gong. He went to the dining room where he was placed at a long table seating perhaps forty people. He recognized among them all his fellow passengers with the exception of young Burnett. A printed menu offered him, besides beef, a choice of bear steak, elk steak, venison, rabbit, wild goose, duck, quail, and snipe. These were on the regular bill. By payment of an extra dollar he could have canned oysters. One fresh egg was fifty cents. Potatoes were fifty cents. He resisted these temptations and ordered bear steak, largely because the sound of it was picturesque. It proved fibrous and strong, but Leslie chewed away on it obstinately, unwilling to confess his mistake.

After the meal he sauntered outside toward the narrow wooden veranda where a row of chairs fronted the night. On his way he was intercepted by a clerk who handed him a folded paper.

I waited a while but did not want to wake you up. [it read] *I am staying with some friends on a rancho and have to go on. But I'll be seeing you in Monterey before long. I'll look you up. And I certainly do appreciate how you stood by. I might have missed my throw, and then I'd have been in a nice fix. That's what my father is going to tell me.*

DJO BURNETT

Leslie read the note under the oil lamp. Djo had, he remembered, assumed that he was on his way to Monterey. That was natural, for Monterey was the stage-line terminus. Now he would not see him again. That was distinctly disappointing. He liked Djo.

The other guests idled by him on their way from the dining room to the bar or to the veranda. Among them

Djo's antagonist, his arm in its sling, was bragging loudly.

"It's a damn lucky thing for him he run away," he was saying to anyone who would listen. "He knows what's good for him. But he'll hear from me yet."

"Better keep out of knife range, Ransom," someone advised him dryly.

"He don't ketch me like that again. Now I *know* he's a rattlesnake. As for that other little whelp——" His eye fell on Leslie. He advanced to within two feet and spread his feet apart truculently. "I got you fixed in my mind, too, young feller, and when I get the use of my arm again I'm going to make it my business to l'arn you to keep out of what ain't your business. Understand me?"

Leslie flushed. He was acutely uncomfortable. The man's bloodshot eyes glared; his jaw was thrust forward belligerently. It was obvious that he was more than half drunk. But his right arm was helpless, and Leslie noted that his holster was still empty. It was not fear that held the young man tongue-tied and embarrassed. Simply that he did not know how he should act in such a situation, and he felt he had a critical audience.

He was relieved of the necessity by the sudden interposition of the doctor. The little man, without the envelopment of his linen duster, was seen to be dressed with exquisite neatness in the height of fashion. He stopped on his way by, arrested by the desperado's vehemence and the expectant group around him. He fixed Ransom with his birdlike black eyes.

"You'd better 'l'arn' yourself to behave and go to bed at once, or you may not have any arm to get the use of," he snapped contemptuously. "What did I tell you about drinking?"

The bigger man wilted ludicrously.

"I only had a few little ones, Doc," he pleaded.

The doctor stared him down, then deliberately produced from his waistcoat pocket an old-fashioned flat snuffbox of silver from which he took a pinch. He held it suspended before him between his thumb and forefinger.

"You've had a dozen," he said flatly. He swept his eyes with a bland and impersonal arrogance over the men standing about. "I don't know whether any of you have any interest whether this man lives or dies," said he. "I'm sure I have not. But if you have, get him to bed." He carried the snuff to his nostrils, turned his back abruptly, hooking his arm through Leslie's.

"Let us enjoy the cool of the evening," he said.

They walked away together.

"I did not suppose he was so badly hurt," said Leslie.

"He isn't badly hurt. But if he drinks, he will have a fever; and if the wound becomes inflamed—that type have none too clean blood."

They sat in two of the wooden chairs on the veranda and tilted back against the wall. The doctor produced two long thin cigars, one of which he offered to Leslie.

"Right. Filthy habit," said he when the young man declined. "I don't recommend it." He lighted the other and puffed comfortably for a few moments in silence.

"None of my business," he said abruptly, "but are you going on tomorrow—on the stage, I mean?"

"Yes."

"That's good. This man Ransom is a good deal of a bully and a braggart, but he is dangerous. I'd hate to see the two of you in the same town."

"Then he's not going on?"

"He thinks he is. But by morning that arm will change his mind for him. Unless he has more physical nerve than I credit him with." The doctor removed the cheroot, looked at the end of it, returned it to his mouth. "I don't want to exaggerate things, but look out for this fellow. He's thoroughly vindictive. He's the kind that does not forget what he considers an injury, and he'll go to considerable lengths to get even. If you ever meet up with him again, keep your eyes open. But he's a coward," he added.

"I will," said Leslie. "Do you know who he is?"

"I've seen him about. I know of him. He's just a sort of professional bad actor. Thug for hire. Political henchman. Shyster lawyer, I understand. Bravo. I don't know what all. Worthless—but dangerous. Now about that thing you wear around your waist." The little man permitted himself a brisk small grin. "You don't impress me as an expert in its use."

Leslie flushed painfully.

"I'm not making fun of you, boy," said the physician kindly, "but let me tell you this: unless you are able to use a revolver quicker and better than the other man, it is much better not to wear one at all. It's just an invitation for trouble."

"That's what my uncle says," said Leslie in a small voice. "Do you advise me not to wear it at all?"

"Your uncle has sense." The doctor turned his eyes quizzically on his embarrassed companion. "None of my business," he repeated. "Needn't incriminate yourself unless you want to, but aren't you the young man who got into a row with Yankee Sullivan?" He chuckled. "Well, you certainly are a connoisseur when it comes to making enemies! I shall follow your career with interest. Now don't mind me." He laid his hand on Leslie's knee. "As a matter of fact, I admire your action keenly. But if you really want my advice, I should say to wear your revolver by all means, but for heaven's sake, to learn to use it. And until you do, just arrange, if you can, to keep it out of the way a little. What think?" He cocked his head sidewise like a bird and laughed. After a moment Leslie, too, laughed, but reluctantly.

III

THE next overnight stop of the stage was at the mission town of San Juan Bautista. True to the doctor's prediction, Ransom remained in San Jose, suffering, it was said, from a fever. Leslie did not see the doctor again. It had not occurred to him to ask the physician whether his business led him farther than San Jose, and the stage left early. Leslie regretted this—as he regretted missing Djo Burnett—but only briefly. The day and the country and the life itself were full of newness and expectation. Both experiences and impressions succeeded each other so rapidly that they must be placed on file, so to speak, for later examination.

At San Juan Bautista, Leslie came for the first time into the preponderantly Spanish. The sleepy little town clustered about the plaza, roughly defined by the dilapidatedly picturesque mission colonnades, the solid square hotel of adobe, and a half-dozen larger two-storied residences of the same material, with second-story balconies running across their fronts. The hotel was thick-walled, dark and cool. The houses were blind and aloof. When the stage had left the following morning, Leslie was the hotel's only guest. The dark-skinned people he encountered, some of them in picturesque costumes that delighted his heart, were courteous enough, responded sufficiently to his direct salutations, but dropped it at that. They were as aloof as the houses on the plaza. Leslie felt himself puzzlingly solitary. He could not realize that San Juan had from the beginning stood in the direct stream of passing; that during the brief period while that stream had eddied with the currents of history every restless adventurer, on both sides, had passed through its dusty ways. Walker and his Mountain Men, Castro, the California revolutionists against Micheltorena, Frémont and his filibusters, and after the Occupation a constant stream of people of all sorts going to and from Monterey or the south. San Juan's natural simplicities had curdled.

Her people had become worldly and sophisticated and suspicious of strangers, for this brief season, before she sank to a forgetfulness which was to endure until, after many years, the automobile again found her out and made her known. Leslie's first impressions, then, of the *californio* were thus wide of the fact and in line with the usual prejudices of his people.

The man to whom he was accredited was a Californian, one Gomez. He, too, was wholly polite and willing to meet the young man's wishes, but he went no further than that. He did not go out of his way to be helpful, nor to correct Leslie's inexperience. Leslie wanted a horse and information as to routes over the mountains to the valley of the Salinas. Señor Gomez sold him a horse and showed him the road over the mountain, adding that he should turn off from the road and up the valley just after he reached the river. He showed no surprise that Leslie wanted but one horse. He did not suggest that the weight of a heavy saddlebag so far back was no fit burden for a riding animal bound on a long journey. He made no mention of the short cut of trail across the slow long lacets of the stage road by which a horseman could save himself time, distance, and dust. His attitude was passive. It was the same with the saddler from whom Leslie bought the rest of his equipment. The picturesqueness of the place had no chance with him. He was glad to get out as quickly as the slow tempo of the people would permit. When finally he rode away it was with a sigh of relief and anticipation.

The mountains immediately back of San Juan were high and rounded and green, with here and there bold outcroppings of sandstone and the dark green of chaparral in cleft and cañon fold. As soon as the little town had dropped from sight, except for the road the country was a primeval wilderness. To be sure the road was sufficient witness to the contrary, for it was rutted deep with the passing of many wheels. But Leslie's youth was quite capable of ignoring a little thing like that. He was alone: there were no witnesses. He was able to enjoy to the full the figure he cut to himself, with his broad flat hat—bought at San Juan—and his Colt's revolving pistol strapped about his waist, and the extraordinary huge-roweled spurs with their tinkling clappers and low-hanging chains at his heels, and the smell of fresh leather and its creak as the horse climbed. He rested his hand on the butt of the Colt's revolving pistol. He practiced drawing the weapon and aiming at things. When he camped he intended to do a little target practice. He spied about him sharply when he happened to think of it, as he supposed a traveler of the wilderness should, though he was a trifle vague in his own mind as for what he spied.

The road mounted steadily by a series of long lacets over the shoulder of the mountain. Leslie followed it conscientiously, unaware of the short cuts across the lacets for a mounted man. It was deeply dusty, but cool small breezes and the dampness of the early-morning air held the dust low and curling along the ground. The valley below flattened to a pattern, and sister mountains across its wide expanse arose steadily, keeping pace.

Toward noon he topped the ridge to look down on the Salinas. Leslie did not know it, but he had made very slow time. He knew little of the management of a horse on a long journey: the animal was overburdened with the weights wrongly distributed. If he were to reach the *casa* of Juan Bardillo where, according to Señor Gomez, he should spend the night, he must mend his pace. Even Leslie, looking down at the distance he must go and back at the distance he had come, realized that. But he did not care. For he had no intention nor desire to sleep at the *casa* of Juan Bardillo. That did not fit the picture at all. From the beginning he had seen himself at the end of this first day's journey sleeping under the stars! The sky his roof! His head on his saddle! The Colt's revolving pistol near his hand! Coyotes on the hill!

2

Youth's ability to ignore what age is pleased to call realities is one of its great assets. The bivouac under the stars was eminently successful, with everything as per schedule, including the coyotes on the hill. There were various things thrown in, such as unexpected lumpiness and hardness of the ground, ants, wood ticks, the horse tangling his picket line, a disconcerting aroma from the saddle blankets Leslie must use as covering, a certain ineptness in the matter of preparing food, and the like. They but scratched the surface of his consciousness without immediate effect.

According to the schedule laid down for him by Señor Gomez, he should by nightfall have reached the mission settlement of Soledad. That, however, assumed considerable diligence in travel, and also that he had spent the previous night with Bardillo. Neither of these things had come off. Indeed Leslie had not passed Bardillo's, nor crossed the river to the Camino Real at all. He had left the road and turned up the valley directly at the foot of the mountains, riding across country. It was much wilder and more romantic that way, preserved for him the illusion of the untouched wilderness. He saw no signs of human habitation, unless occasional bands of long-horned wild-looking cattle might be so considered. On the other hand, quail, rabbits, and mourning doves swarmed; coyotes sat on their haunches to stare at him speculatively, their tongues hanging drolly like dogs; twice a wildcat scrambled away through the thin low brush; once, to his great excitement, for he was city bred, he flushed a deer from the bottom land of a ravine. The animal was not much alarmed, so it leaped away in a series of leisurely high bounces, tucking its legs neatly at the top of each leap, as though suspended from a spiral spring. Leslie half drew the pistol from its holster but dropped it back, urged to prudence by a very suspicious slant to his horse's ear. Once he thought he saw a bear far up the slope of the hill, but he could not be quite certain. However, the mere chance that it might be a bear was exciting. The whole journey was eminently satisfactory. Oddly enough Leslie came the nearest to dissatisfaction over the red-winged blackbirds and meadowlarks: they were too much like the blackbirds and meadowlarks he was accustomed to back home. They somehow diluted the wilderness.

However, by late afternoon the first fine rapture began to wear just a little thinner. Leslie's objective contemplation of the appearance he cut was not so absorbing. He knew intimately what he looked like. The Colt's revolving pistol was very heavy at his waist, which was natural, for he had strapped it close to his body instead of allowing it to hang more loosely at his hips. Finally he took it off and strapped it to his saddle horn. He began to get a trifle saddle weary, muscle sore from the unaccustomed riding, chafed on the inside of his knees. He shifted position often. The sun was powerful. The broken rest of the night before began to assert itself.

Nevertheless Leslie continued to ride. He had with him sufficient provision for another night in the open, but the thought of a bed and a square meal had begun to possess a certain appeal. Soledad could not be so very much farther. Leslie peered ahead hopefully from the top of each small crest of the gently rolling valley, but in vain. He saw the dark high mountains to the south, the lower grass-grown ranges close to his left hand, the wide valley between, the wandering green of the river's cottonwoods. The sun had dipped low, and the young man had begun seriously to consider another bivouac, when he caught a glimpse of white beyond live oaks and the red tiles of a roof. An outpost of Soledad at last, he reflected with satisfaction, and put his tired and overburdened horse to a jouncing trot.

But as he drew into plainer sight he reined in again. This was not Soledad, but a solitary small *rancho*.

Leslie debated with himself. He had seen little of the Spanish Californian. The idle, swaggering, vicious riffraff of the San Francisco gambling houses plus the aloof and lazy-looking street loafers at San Juan had given him a bad impression of the race and had endorsed the loose "shiftless-greaser" talk of the city. He did not quite know whether he wanted to show himself or not.

The matter was taken out of his decision by the opening of a door and the shouting of a greeting. He had then, in common decency, to ride forward.

3

Soledad was far, much too far. But no, it must not be thought of. The *caballero* must stop the night. *Mañana,* yes; *mañana,* then was time enough for that; and he, Tomas Valdez, would put the señor on his way.

So Tomas Valdez; and a flood more of musical syllables that Leslie's slight Spanish could not completely grasp: but the purport was plain, and the flash of the man's teeth was friendly; and behind him a comfortably plump woman, with parted blue-black hair sleek as a seal and wonderful soft eyes, smiled too; and a welter of small children and lank dogs pressed close behind her; and a glimpse through the doorway of red flames in the interior's darkness. Leslie felt suddenly weary and acquiescent. He dismounted stiffly, lifting his leg above the overstuffed saddlebags only with the greatest difficulty. Scarcely had he touched foot to ground before two lads of twelve or fourteen years had taken the horse in charge. One tossed the heavy stirrup across the saddle, undid the cinch, whisked the saddle with one deft motion from the horse's back.

"Ai-ee!" he whistled softly as he felt its weight. He turned, half carrying, half dragging it through the doorway of the house. The other boy led away the horse.

"My house and all that it contains is yours," said Tomas Valdez with a grand flourish.

The interior of the house was bare. The floor was of earth, watered and beaten hard. Across one corner was a conical-shaped open fireplace. In another corner was a heap of dried rawhides and a pile of wheat. In the center of the room stood two benches, one higher than the other; the higher might have been called a table. Around the adobe wall had been built, of the same material, a low shelf or bench which was used, apparently, as a seat or a bed or a store shelf as need arose. From the heavy beams overhead hung a guitar, a violin, and strings of bright red peppers.

Leslie took his place at the bench table with Tomas Valdez. Señora Valdez brought food. The various-sized children sat on the floor or the adobe shelf and stared avidly.

In every detail of the entertainment of that evening was almost a poverty of simplicity. Señora Valdez wore merely a white cambric robe, loosely belted; was without shoes or stockings, without ornament except for a few silver rings. The very youngest children wore nothing; the elder girls merely a single garment; the elder boys a loose shirt and trousers. Tomas Valdez had, it appeared, somewhat more pretension to elegance. He had on a loose shirt, a small sleeveless jacket, *calzoneras* of cotton velvet, leggings and shoes of soft leather, but all threadbare and much worn. The woman served in unglazed earthenware vessels some stewed jerked meat with chilis, tortillas, and a hot drink resembling coffee. There was no table furniture. Leslie discovered he must use his fingers and his knife. He copied his host carefully, and when he had finished he wiped his knife blade and mopped out the inside of his bowl with the last of the tortillas, swallowed the latter. He arose to present the bowl to his hostess.

"*Muchas gracias, señora,*" he pronounced carefully.

The woman's brown face broke into a delightful smile. "*Buen' provecho, señor,*" she returned.

His hosts piled bright *serapes* on the adobe shelf for his seat. Themselves sat at either hand. They talked to him, slowly and distinctly for his easy comprehension, smiling at him encouragingly, their manners gentle with an exquisite courtesy. They asked him no questions about himself, though Valdez was very inquisitive as to the effect of the new American government, which he seemed to favor. Or that might be courtesy, reflected Leslie.

"I like the Americans," said Valdez. "I refused, myself, to join the revolt."

Especially he and the woman quizzed Leslie as to the effect of the new dispensation on the prices of the few things they used.

"This," said Señora Valdez, fingering her gown, "cost us twelve dollars."

"That," interposed Valdez, "is eight skins of the cow."

"Do you think that the *americanos* will sell it more cheaply?"

Stampede

Leslie did not know much of such things, but he had seen the shopwindows in Philadelphia.

"I do not know. But in my home such a dress sells for about three," said he.

"Ai-ee!" cried Señora Valdez. "To think of that!"

She disappeared to return immediately with her arms filled. She waited anxiously for Leslie's appraisal of all the various items of her meager wardrobe. He guessed rather wildly at some things, it must be confessed. The Señora Valdez clapped her hands, her fine eyes alight; she was as vivacious as a girl.

"See, Tomas!" she cried. "Soon under the Americans we shall become *hidalgo!*"

It cost, under the old regime, they both explained together, upward of two hundred cattle to clothe a man genteelly, just for a suit of clothes. How much for a suit of clothes in the señor's country? Leslie did not know: Americans did not wear the same kind of clothes; sixty dollars, perhaps.

The two looked at one another, breathless, like children.

"Forty cows!" cried Señora Valdez.

Tomas took down the violin and guitar from the beams overhead. He and the eldest boy played. They all sang.

The instrumental pieces were lively, always, but the songs were plaintive and sometimes sad. After a time Tomas conducted Leslie to a smaller room in which was a low bedframe laced with rawhide thongs. Only by next morning's daylight did he find out that this was the only other room of the house and that the couple must have turned over to him their own sleeping quarters. He accused them of it. They merely smiled and spread their hands.

The breakfast was a repetition of the supper. Outside Leslie saw only a conical clay bake oven and extensive corrals of greasewood stakes. Nothing else. No more possessions. Yet somehow he carried with him as he rode away an impression of space and magnificence. He tried to offer money for his entertainment. Tomas Valdez refused.

"Señor," said he with dignity, "I am not in the habit of selling food."

4

Somehow the incident was, to Leslie, like the passing through a door into a new country with new inhabitants. Thenceforward he rode in Old California as it had always been, and the new febrile order of things was over the horizon. This was quite as interesting to his enthusiasms as had been his illusion of wilderness, so he ceased riding cross country and veered over to the Camino Real, courting now, rather than avoiding, chance encounters. There was not much travel along the old highway, but sufficient. He passed an Indian with bound straight hair driving oxen to a shrieking *carreta* piled with hides; a brown-frocked priest on a mule; two *vaqueros* with flat glazed hats tied under their chins and broad leathern leg aprons, who whirled past in charge of a band of high-headed, wild-looking horses; a gentleman and his lady who ambled by, *paso lento*, very gay and gorgeous in silver and velvet and broadcloth, and the caparisons of their horses tinkling with silver bells. These all looked at him with veiled curiosity, for Leslie's appearance and equipment were strange and unreasonable to them, but they concealed their astonishment gravely and greeted him with sonorous courtesy:

"*Buenos días, señor*"; and as they passed, "*Vaya con Dios!*"

And Leslie recalled what, among other things, the little doctor at San Jose had told him:

"As soon as you get into the Spanish country you will be perfectly safe from the road agents. Until then watch out a bit. There are here and there quite a number of outlaws disguised as Californians. You can generally be sure of them, for a genuine native always salutes you and would do so were his hand on the trigger of his pistol to kill you the next moment."

Leslie became a little self-conscious because of the big Colt's pistol. He ended by bestowing it in one of the *cantinas,* out of sight.

He stopped overnight at the vast and gloomy fortress-like Mission of Our Lady of Soledad. Like most of the other missions, it had by now fallen into disrepair, and its ancient wealth was gone. Nevertheless it was still maintained meagerly as a church. Leslie was given a bare clean room in the guest wing, was fed in the silent refectory, and was blessed at his departure. Except at the meal and at arrival and departure, he had no company. The two priests had business of their own, and the Indian servant who attended his few wants made him no answers. Little bells tinkled, and at vespers the great bells in the tower spoke. Leslie slipped into the dimness of the church, partly from a sense of fitting courtesy, partly from curiosity. The last light of day slanted milky from windows high up near the roof; candle flames in galaxy glorified the altar; sweet-smelling smoke eddied; on the high walls were crude paintings of sinners waist deep in hell flames;

a scant dozen dark figures kneeled. That night Leslie lay for some time flat on his back, staring straight up into the blackness of his cell. About him was a comfortable peace like the waters of a bath. He heard a rapid, soft-voiced little owl repeating something breathlessly and a commanding hollow-voiced big owl telling the world of night. Some small metronomic insect went *tick-tick-tick* in the beams overhead. A far bell tinkling attested a ceaseless vigilance against the powers of darkness.

IV

BOTH Leslie and his much-tried horse left Soledad quite made over to a new and strange and delightful world. Here, too, offer of payment had been refused, but Leslie had caught sight of a contribution box by the door of the church, and his conscience was clear. In addition to a Latin blessing, he had received at parting a provision of food and minute directions as to the next stage of his journey, which was to the Mission of St. Anthony of Padua on the plateau of Jolon. The *hacienda* of Don José Constansio, to whom he was accredited, lay but a few leagues beyond. There was no reason, said Father Feria, why he should not, with proper diligence, reach the mission by night, and his destination the following day.

Leslie thanked him kindly and rode away. He had, however, no intention of using proper diligence. The two nights' sound rest had so refreshed him that the under-the-stars, open-sky-for-his-roof appeal had revived.

So now he rode slowly and stopped frequently and looked about him from a center of vast leisure on the varied phenomena of an interesting world. Much of it was wholly strange and, therefore, romantic. The increasing abundance of stately and soaring eagles, for one thing. Leslie had not yet been told the birds were in reality buzzards, so they did well enough for the purpose. Then there were spiders, unbelievably large, with hairy bodies, that teetered up and down on their legs as though about to spring. And iridescent lizards like jewels that made him quaint little bows. And a flat, wide reptile that looked as though it had swallowed a particularly spiky rosebush and the thorns had come out through its hide. And scorpions. And magpies. These were all, to Leslie, exotics. He experienced, on beholding them, the same thrill of the unbelievable he had felt at sight of his first orange tree or his first fresh figs. There is a certain opening of the doors of consciousness when we encounter face to face what has been only a legend. So Leslie rode that day in a constantly mounting delight, not only in the rising green country of hills and spaced dark oaks, but in the numbers of little things the simplicity of that country contained. His appreciations were heightened by this quickening of consciousness. He expanded and soaked up and had a grand time.

His horse suddenly leaped sideways, shaking him loose in the saddle. This was a curious enough phenomenon, for the horse was by now somewhat subdued by its troubles. Leslie saw something wriggling away through the grass. He looked closer. There was no doubt of it! A rattlesnake! In person!

He scrambled from the saddle, hastily tied the animal to the nearest willow bush, gave pursuit. He wanted that snake's skin on his hat. But by this time the reptile had disappeared.

Leslie was recalled from eager but cautious search by a snort. He looked up to confront a wide-horned steer trotting toward him from the brush. The beast's head was high and swinging from side to side; its eye was rolling, wild but foolish. Leslie waved his hat and shouted. The beast snorted again, stopped short. After a moment it advanced again, nor did another shout nor the stone Leslie

Stampede

cast in its direction have any other effect than to check its pace slightly.

Leslie, though city bred, as cities went nearly a hundred years ago, knew cows well enough back East, where he came from; and it did not yet occur to him that his predicament was anything but annoying. Even when the brute lowered its horns and rushed at him and he was forced to dodge, his emotion was of indignation at stupidity. But when the steer turned to come again, with every indication of serious and purposeful business, Leslie suddenly realized he was in a fix.

The next two or three minutes hammered into him just how serious that fix was. By continued shouting, leaping about, and casting of stones and clods of earth he could for a little time hold the beast, if not at bay, at least in a condition of dull uncertainty. But sooner or later its tail lashed, down went its head, and at him it came, full tilt in a short purposeful rush which he but just managed to evade. He tried to edge over toward a tree but instantly discovered that the least yielding brought an instant charge. He wished he had the Colt's revolving pistol. He wished his horse were nearer. He wondered how long the fool animal would keep this up. The consequences of a stumble or a fall tightened his muscles. He was hot, and his breath was beginning to come short. But as yet no real fear of the outcome had crossed his mind. That came when, in a pause of this absurd game, he looked beyond his antagonist and saw more cattle, a great ring of them, just at the edge of the brush that bordered the meadow. They were staring at the strange performance taking place out there in the open, making up their slow minds as to what it was all about, but avidly curious. They stood motionless, held by this indecision; but the thought came to Leslie, like a cold blade through his chest, that once their stupidity was focused he was as surely doomed as though he stood on the roof of a burning building. Only there would be some sense and fitness in the danger of such a predicament, and it could be accepted with a due sense of tragedy; but in this there was none. But he knew desperately that unless he did something within the next minute or so to escape this one animal, he had no chance at all to escape the many.

He remembered the little double-barreled derringer, which he had bestowed in a pocket, and produced it and took careful aim and popped it off. Leslie could not expect the tiny bullets to take any serious effect, but he had a faint hope their sting might discourage the steer's tenacity. If they hit, which he seriously doubted, they had no effect; nor did the explosions accomplish anything. Except that the ring of cattle at the meadow's edge stirred slightly and two or three made tentative steps forward. Leslie tightened his muscles for a dash toward safety. It would be a forlorn chance: he was almost certain to be overtaken and trampled down, but he must take it. Curiously enough a wave of rage overwhelmed him that he should meet his end ridiculously.

But at this moment a rider thrust from the brush screen at his left and loped easily across the meadow. The steer rolled its bloodshot eyes and shook its head slowly from side to side.

Leslie saw that the rider was a girl.

"Guardarse!" he cried in warning. *"El toro e barbaro!"* He could not for the life of him summon the Spanish word for "dangerous."

She did not even glance in his direction. Quite unhurriedly she cantered directly at the steer. The brute stared, holding its ground more in the slow stupidity of changing ideas than in defiance. The girl flicked the end of her romal in the animal's face.

"Hola!" she cried sharply.

Overcome by the sudden panic of its race-long subservience to the mounted man, the steer abruptly whirled and lumbered away. She watched it thoughtfully, then, as though seized by a sudden impulse, she leaned forward in her saddle and spoke sharply to her horse.

The steer, running swiftly, had by now almost reached his companions at the brush edge. But in a dozen leaps the horse was alongside. Its rider leaned from her saddle in a long graceful sweep, caught the steer's tail. The horse, without command, sprang forward violently. The intended maneuver, had Leslie known it, was the *colliar*. Its suddenness, combined with a certain deftness in the application of the power, should have turned the steer end for end, to his great discomfiture and his edification as to his proper place in the scheme of things. But the beast was much too heavy for the girl's strength. She hung on until she was almost dragged from the saddle before, with a cry of vexation, she was forced to let go. The steer was slewed only slightly sidewise, but as it bawled loudly with terror, possibly the ends of the *colliar* were subserved. She straightened in her saddle and rode away without a backward glance.

Leslie watched all this with openmouthed astonishment. Only when the beautiful golden bay animal and the slim straight figure of its rider were fairly at the point of disappearance in the chaparral did he come to himself

Stampede 69

in the realization that his rescuer actually intended to ride off thus without a word.

"Hey!" he yelled as a stopgap in his frantic search for Spanish. *"Señorita! S'il vous plaît*—damn it, that's French! Oh hell and blazes! *Volver usted!"*

The horse stopped short, but its rider did not turn. Leslie collected himself, uttered a more grammatically correct plea. Slowly the horse wheeled, paced steadily across the carpet of flowers.

2

Leslie had leisure to see that his rescuer was a young girl—hardly more than a child, he would have said had he himself been older. She rode a very fine golden bay whose skin rippled and shone in the sunlight, molding the muscles and the network of veins like gold leaf. A headstall of silver plates and *conchas* and a saddle carved and ornamented would have merited attention—at another time. It was a man's saddle, and the girl rode it astride. Her hat also was a man's hat, tied under her chin by a thong. Her costume was of red and the blue of lupins; red above and blue in a sort of divided skirt below. Leslie did not know it, of course, but in such a rig-out on a proper *doncellita* of the period he was looking upon something quite as revolutionary as Bunker Hill. Of this privilege, however, he was blandly ignorant. He knew only that this was a very good-looking young lady and that she was staring at him with what seemed to be grave and steady disapproval. To his smile she made no response, but waited, from that elevation of superiority one mounted possesses over one on foot, for what he might say.

"I could not allow you to go away without thanking you," he ventured in his halting Spanish.

"No ay de qui," she disclaimed briefly and continued to wait.

"I am afraid I would not make a very good bullfighter, not a good *matador*."

She continued to look down on him coolly.

Leslie realized quite well the ridiculous figure he must have cut in the eyes of this very competent young person to whom man-eating cows were nothing. Nevertheless, ridiculous or not, he knew well she had saved him from death, and he was determined to jar her out of this inhuman aloofness, to make her know that he understood this fact. He tried to tell her so, and especially to express admiration for her handling of the belligerent steer. Her face flushed slightly under its olive pallor. Her eyes lost none of their steadiness, but they glinted with an anger

Stampede

Leslie could not mistake. He was bewildered. He knew nothing of the *colliar* and could not guess her failure, nor her secret mortification. He wondered what he could have said; in what manner the strange language had betrayed him.

She looked away at last. Some of the cattle were again venturing from the chaparral.

"I think," said she, "you'd better get hold of your horse, before you get into any more trouble."

"Good Lord!" cried Leslie when he had managed to shut his mouth. "You speak English!"

"And why not?" she demanded haughtily.

"Why—no reason—except that it is rather unexpected —back here so far—a Spanish girl," Leslie stammered, taken aback by her prickly challenge. He recovered himself. "Look here, now that I can talk without thinking of a dictionary, I want to tell you that I know that you came along just in time to save my life, and I'm no end grateful. It was silly of me to get into such a fix, I suppose, but I didn't know anything about your confounded cattle and their silly customs. I'm new to the country." A new thought crossed his mind. "Are you understanding me?" he asked.

Leslie received an instant impression that if the girl had not been mounted, she would have stamped her foot.

"Will you tell me," she said in the tone of exasperation, "what there is about what you are saying that I could not understand? Of course you are new to the country, and of course you are foolish. Otherwise you would not go on foot where there are cattle."

Leslie remembered the little derringer pistol that he still held in his hand.

"Are these your cattle? Do you live here?" he asked on a sudden thought. "I do not think I hurt the beast; I do not think I hit it at all."

She dismissed the matter with a wave of the hand. She was examining him steadily, making up her mind about something, Leslie could see. Her eyes strayed to his meekly patient horse that stood, ears drooped, one hind foot tucked up, hoping for the best. They rested on the beast for some moments, taking in every detail of its equipment, the bulky *cantinas* over the horn, the stuffed saddlebags behind the cantle. Here, said they—could Leslie have read them—is probably as complete a greenhorn as ever rode abroad in Alta California. Not only does he go about among wild cattle on foot, where only a mounted man is safe, but also he ties his horse by the bridle reins, and he loads a heavy weight behind the saddle where it will most certainly result in a sore back. It is probable that he knows nothing about the *colliar,* and therefore he was not making fun of my failure to execute it properly.

Leslie could not read all that, but he read well enough the change of mood, and he responded to it with all the cheerful abandon of a puppy. With a sure instinct, however, he carefully repressed all evidences of joy beneath a sudden formal correctness.

"My name, señorita"—he bowed—"is Leslie Dayton, and I am journeying to the *rancho of* Don José Constansio."

"Señor," she murmured in acknowledgment.

"And you?" he hinted, as she did not immediately reciprocate but appeared to consider some inner problem.

She recollected herself with a start.

"I? Your pardon, señor. I am the Doña Amata of the *rancho* of Folded Hills. And this," she added gravely, "is Pronto, who is quite the best horse in the world." Pronto, undoubtedly in response to some touch of heel or other signal which Leslie did not see, bent one knee, lowered his glossy head, and sank into a half obeisance. She broke into a gurgle of delighted laughter. It came to Leslie suddenly that she was indeed a child. Or was she? She was very puzzling.

She gathered up the reins and turned Pronto's head.

"Come," she ordered with decision. "Oh, the *pobrecito!*" she cried of Leslie's dejected animal.

"What's the matter?" he asked in all innocence.

He received a severe small lecture.

"I didn't know," he said contritely. "I'll get another horse."

He had a brilliant idea.

"Can't I buy one at your place?" he asked. "How far away is it?" He caught the recoil of doubt. "Come on," he pleaded; "anyway it's a long way to San Antonio yet. I ought not to try—now should I?—with that horse; and anyway how about all this California hospitality they talk so much about? Are you going to let the stranger pass right by your very doorstep without asking him———"

"Stop! Stop!" She covered her ears with her gauntleted hands. "So many words! You do not understand! How would it look; what would *mi madre* say that I should speak to a young man, a stranger? And if I bring him with me—no! No, no!" In her excitement she became Latin for the first time. "And besides———"

"Yes? Besides?" prompted Leslie as she hesitated.

She flushed faintly, glanced down.

"My costume, my saddle. That would be a scandal."

"What's the matter with it? It's a very pretty costume, a very fine saddle."

Stampede

Leslie learned that ladies did not ride astride; that the Doña Amata was already somewhat of a scandal to *"mi madre"* and one Vicenta because she continued to do so so late in life even though the shame were performed only in the supposed strict privacy of the fifty-odd thousand acres of Folded Hills. "Though," added Amata in aside, "my father only laughs." If she were now to appear, openly, riding with a strange young man . . .

"But if your father only laughs," urged Leslie, "and after all, you can sort of *bring* me in, can't you?"

"But *mi madre* . . ." The girl bit her lip in hesitation.

"Mothers," said Leslie confidently, "are my specialty." He composed his face to an incredible wide-eyed innocence. " 'Señora, I have come to pay my respects in gratitude to your daughter who has, in the goodness of her heart, rescued me from an untimely and disagreeable fate. She did this against all her better inclinations, much as one would pick a skunk out of a mud hole, actuated only by her good heart which, señora, she undoubtedly inherited from you.' Hold on!" He broke off in alarm. "Does your mother understand English?"

"Why, of course she does!" cried the Doña Amata indignantly.

"That's good. I'm not at my best in Spanish. Well, and

so forth and so on. I'll handle your mother. Don't you worry about her. I'm a lot more scared of your father—even if he does laugh. You're sure he doesn't bite?"

"Doesn't bite!" the girl repeated and gurgled deliciously. "You say funny things."

"They'd be a lot funnier in Spanish," stated Leslie confidently. "Do I have to talk Spanish to your father?"

"My father!" She widened her eyes in amazement. "Talk Spanish? To my father? Why, my father is *americano!*"

Leslie struck his forehead in mock vexation.

"The poor dumb fish!" he cried.

"What is it?" She leaned down from her saddle in puzzled alarm.

"You talk English without an accent—beautiful English," said Leslie reproachfully. "You live in the Salinas valley—on a *rancho*. What did you say is the name of the *rancho?*"

"Folded Hills." She stared at him, puzzled.

"Of course. And your father is an American. All laid out in front of one, plain as print! And I've just guessed it! Young woman"—he raised a forefinger as though in accusation—"your name is Burnett, and you have a brother named Djo."

"For sure." Her voice was wondering. "Did I not tell you that?"

"You did not!"

"But you asked, and I did tell you my name."

"You said your name is Amata—which is a very good name—and you quit at that."

"That was stupid," she acknowledged. "Such is the Spanish custom to name one's name thus."

"George, rex," said Leslie.

"What?" She knit her brows.

"Nothing. But such being the case—that you are Djo's sister, I mean—the goose hangs high. You see, Djo is a friend of mine."

She looked at him doubtfully.

"What's the matter?" he asked. "Don't you believe it? Djo will know me."

"Djo is at Monterey."

"That's too bad. I'd like to see him."

"And if he comes back and finds you here—as his friend——" She hesitated, flushing. "I do not like troubles," she said with simple dignity.

Leslie threw back his head and roared with delighted laughter. She looked at him doubtfully, broke into a reluctant smile.

"But I *do* know him," choked Leslie at last. "Honest Injun, cross my heart, hope to die! And I hope he does come back from Monterey!"

3

When the two surmounted the hill and looked down into the valley where was located the *casa* of the ranch, Leslie drew rein with a whistle of surprise.

"Golly!" he exclaimed.

Directly below them the fields of the valley were green with ripening crops of wheat and barley. At the far side of the flats were wide patches of garden—*milpas*—and orderly rows of fruit trees. On the slopes sprawled the spring shoots of an extensive vineyard. A meandering line of green trees marked a watercourse. At the upper end of the valley was a whole series of corrals and chutes of all sizes, indicative of the *rancho's* major industry. Beyond them, on the upper grassy slope, grazed a band of horses.

Across the way, nestled comfortably between two huge live-oak trees, was a long, low white structure with a red-tiled roof. It occupied the whole top of a knoll. Falling away from it on the descending slope were innumerable other buildings of various sizes, scattered apparently at haphazard, until, in a lesser flat a few hundred yards distant, they clustered into a certain loose semblance of a village.

Leslie looked toward the girl, impressed. Her slight figure stood upright in the stirrups; her head was back; her eyes and nostrils were wide with an obvious pride.

"Folded Hills *rancho*," she said simply.

V

They rode down into the flat of the valley and across it and up the gentle slope to the great live-oak trees. Here they drew rein. The girl cried out sharply, and after a few moments an Indian *mozo* sauntered around the grape arbor and took the horses. In the man's face was no expression, but his black eyes were alight with curiosity. Without apparent movement their glance roved over every detail of the young man's appearance and equipment, and a certain faint astonishment grew in their depths. Of this the Doña Amata was well enough aware, and her head went up.

"Is Don Andreo in the *casa?*" she demanded imperiously.

"The Don Andreo rides, señorita." The *mozo* hesitated. "The señor's luggage?" he inquired. "In the west room?"

"Leave it here," commanded the girl, "under the oak. Come! Hasten!"

The *mozo* unstrapped the *cantinas,* the saddlebags, deposited them under the oak, led the horses away at a brisk pace. The girl looked after him and laughed.

"I must go find *Mamá* at once; for quick, like that!" she snapped her fingers. "This news will be brought to her, and I must see her first. Will you wait? I shall not be long. Will you come into the *casa?*"

"I think I would like to wait here, if you don't mind," said Leslie.

He watched her slender figure until it had disappeared through the cavernous doorway between incredibly tall hollyhocks. She moved lightly and gracefully, as he would expect. Two benches stood under the nearer of the great oaks. He sat down on one of them and took off his hat.

It was very pleasant in the cool of shade after the ardent sunshine. A breeze lifted his hair. Small busy birds searched the foliage of the wide-flung branches and talked in confidential twitters of their own world in which he had little part. Concealed in the top, a dove mourned softly over and over. From the drench of sunshine outside came other, warmed sounds of quail and meadowlark, of voices muted by distance, a sharp tinkle of something metal falling, a far-off repeated bellowing of cattle. These sounds were busy, but here in the somnolent shade of the tree was only a soft and droning quietude. Leslie fell under its spell. He was quite content to wait. His eyes wandered with a lazy and sensuous appreciation over the bright tall flowers of the garden strip along the walls of the *casa* and the shadows they cast against the white. His nostrils expanded to their faint perfume mingled with an equally faint tang of wood smoke. The house spread out so comfortably, as though relaxing against the earth. Leslie's own eyes drooped; his head nodded.

An earthen jar suspended from a limb by a thong of rawhide swung and turned slowly. Its surface was bedewed with moisture. To avoid falling asleep Leslie arose idly to investigate it. Its mouth was closed by a wooden cover. On the cover was a cup. Leslie drank of the water it contained and was astounded to find it cold as ice.

He sat down again. Amata was a long time in finding her mother; or perhaps, Leslie reflected with a grin, in making her peace. He hoped there was no trouble. Why should there be? But he knew nothing of these Spanish people, except that he had heard they were very strict and punctilious. But these weren't Spanish people. Or were they? In ideas, that is. I'd like mighty well to stay here, reflected Leslie. It is restful. And beautiful. I'd like to see Djo again. I liked Djo. Funny way to spell Joe. His thoughts for some reason avoided the girl, glancing at her only obliquely, as it were. He spared a passing speculation as to her age. You couldn't tell a thing, the way she was dressed. There were rare odd moments when somehow she gave the impression of being nothing but a little girl.

Leslie heard the sound of hoofs and looked up. In his inner absorption the horsemen had ridden up the hill unnoticed and were now close upon him. The one slightly in advance was to Leslie's boyish eyes a splendid figure of a man. Certainly he was splendidly mounted. The beast he rode was above the average of size for the country, of a light chestnut in color. Its mane and tail were long and silky and had overnight been so tightly braided that now they flashed in deep ripples that caught the light. The animal's forehead was wide, its eyes intelligent; its widespread nostrils showed pink as the light shone through them. It stepped daintily, as though in pride.

The harness was befitting such a creature. The bridle and reins were of plaited rawhide, the crossing of the straps marked by silver *conchas*. The broad sides of the spade bit were silver inlaid and engraved; silver chains connected it with the reins. The saddle rested on a gaudy Indian blanket. It was a massive affair, with a high, wide pommel and broad skirts, the leather deeply and beautifully tooled, the corners silvered. The leathern stirrup hoods were extended downward in long points—*tapaderos*—that all but touched the ground.

Magnificent a show as all this presented, Leslie's attention lingered on it but a moment. The man dominated it, compelled his first interest. He was tall, spare rather than slender. Except for the wide hat and the big-roweled spurs, he was dressed soberly in American costume. He sat very straight in his saddle, his legs fully extended and well beneath him. His body was supple, moved in response to every slight movement of the horse. His face was lean and set in lines of determination. His eyes were of a clear hard gray, and above them the brows almost met in a straight line. This assured the resemblance, so that Leslie knew he saw Djo's father—and, incidentally, the father of the girl.

So wholly was his interest focused on this man that for

several paces of the advance he did not look at the other two riders. When he did finally turn his eyes to them, surprise brought him to his feet. One was a *vaquero* of late middle age. The third horseman was the man named Ransom, the loud-mouthed bullying desperado with whom Djo Burnett had clashed on the stage journey to San Jose.

2

Leslie moved out of sight behind the bole of the live-oak tree. He needed a moment to recall his scattered wits before confronting the man. What was he after here? Djo? That was not reasonable: he would hardly have ridden in alone and so openly if he had been on any errand of ordinary personal revenge. It was ridiculous to suppose that he had come thus far to complain of Djo to his father, as one who complains of a small boy who steals his apples. It was equally ridiculous that, in view of what had passed, he should suppose himself welcome here on any basis.

Unless he knew that Djo was still at Monterey.

Leslie's young imagination quickened. What then? What was he up to? What did he hope to accomplish here while Djo was still away? While he still remained unknown? Something deep and dastardly and revengeful, without doubt. Worm his way into the *ranchero's* confidence, so that when the time came . . . The plot became a trifle hazy at this point, but one fact stuck solidly enough: here was he, Leslie, to step forth dramatically in confrontation when the time came. If the man's dark plots needed anonymity, he had another guess coming. Leslie listened shamelessly.

However, the first exchange he heard, after the men had dismounted, rather knocked the props from under part of the theory. If Ransom intended to worm his way into the *ranchero's* confidence, he made a bad start. His manner was almost arrogantly confident. He produced from an inside pocket an envelope containing a number of papers. He selected and unfolded one, referred to it as though to refresh his memory.

"You acknowledge yourself then as Andrew Burnett?" he demanded.

Andy surveyed him from beneath frowning brows.

"I am Andrew Burnett, as I told you," he answered at last.

"You lay claim," continued Ransom, again referring to the document in his hand, "to that piece of land designated as Folded Hills *rancho* comprising eleven leagues *poco mas o meno'?*"

"I own Folded Hills ranch," said Andy curtly. His lips were compressed, his eyes wary.

Ransom restored the papers to his pocket.

"You will produce your title papers and your *diseño*," said he, "and will designate someone—or come yourself—as my assistant to identify the boundary marks."

The tall *ranchero* sauntered to the nearest bench and sat down.

"Why should I do this?" he asked at length.

"I am a United States officer," stated Ransom importantly.

Andy nodded.

"I guessed that. Though I'll let you show me. What I asked you is why I'm to do these things? What's the idea?"

"Checking your title. If it's good, you got nothing to get skeered of. If it ain't, the gov'ment wants to know it. There's aplenty wants land," he ended significantly.

Andy remained silent, pondering. The other watched him, a slight sneer on his lips.

"There's no use bucking the gov'ment, if that's what you're thinking of."

"I'm not thinking of bucking the government," said Andy, "but I want to get this straight."

Leslie stepped from his concealment behind the tree.

"How are you, Ransom?" he said coolly. "Didn't expect to see you here. You're too late. I'm doing this job."

His voice was without tremor, but his heart was jumping with the excitement of his inspiration and the course he must hold. He was conscious of the *ranchero's* steady tight-lipped scrutiny. He threw at Andy a smile that he tried to make at once one of amused and shrewd understanding and an appeal for discretion. This was rather complicated. But as Andy still said nothing, Leslie plucked up heart.

Ransom, on the contrary, was vocal enough.

"You!" he cried. "For God's sake! How did *you* get here!"

"You're too late," repeated Leslie. "I'm doing this job." He spoke quickly: he must get on before the *ranchero* might say something. "I'm nearly finished."

"What are you driveling about now?" Ransom caught his breath.

"I, too," said Leslie grandly, "am a Federal Land Inspector."

It was a great moment, but still perilous with possibili-

Stampede

ties; and Leslie's artistic perception felt somehow that the method of his disclosure smacked perhaps too strongly of the theatrical. Nevertheless it was effective. Andy Burnett's lips closed in a straight line; his eyes moved sharply from one to the other; he waited, saying nothing.

"The hell you are!" said Ransom contemptuously.

Leslie unstrapped his saddlebags, produced his commission with the red seal, thrust it under Ransom's nose. The latter's eyes opened wide with surprise. However, he brushed its importance aside with a contemptuous gesture.

"I got orders to examine this title, and I'm going to do it," said he. "I don't know how you got a hold of that appointment, and I don't care. I been in this business too long to bother about no young whippersnapper like you are. Who told you to come here, anyway? I'll take this over. You can give me what you've done. Or," he ended violently, "you can go to hell. Anyway, get out!"

His face was red and congested; his hand strayed, a little stiffly, toward the butt of his weapon. Leslie found leisure for a brief regret that the Colt's revolving pistol was in the *cantinas* and the derringer in his pocket empty. But he did not recede; and indeed his fears would have been groundless, for Ransom's movement was purely instinctive. He was angry enough, but he knew better than to start a gunplay on a lone hand.

"You are not my superior," he told Ransom bluntly. "You cannot give me orders."

The disputants turned at the sound of Andy's voice. To Leslie's surprise the *ranchero's* eyes were twinkling with amusement.

"That'll be about all, Ransom—if that's your name," he drawled. "This young man says he's nigh finished with the job. That's fast workin'. I like fast work. I'm satisfied."

He arose with an air of finality.

"You deny a gov'ment officer?" cried Ransom, beside himself.

"Why, no"—Andy opened his eyes mildly—"but I've *got* me a government officer. I don't have to have two, do I?" His voice took on an edge; his tall form straightened. "Or do I? How about that, young man? You tell me."

"No," said Leslie boldly. "This man has no standing!"

"Why, you——" burst out Ransom. He gave it up and turned on Andy. "Look here, I've got orders, definite orders, I tell you, to examine this title, and I——"

"There's your hoss," interrupted Andy bluntly. "I never aimed to turn a man from Folded Hills without feeding him, but, Ransom, I don't like your face, or your manners, or anything about you." The man broke in with something about Federal officers and authority. "I don't know anything about that," said Andy with finality, "but when I got two of these yere Federal officers, and one says one thing, and t'other says another, I'm going to pick me the one I want to believe. It ain't you. Vamoose!"

3

Beaming with pleasure that his inspiration had worked out so well and that the *ranchero* had not given the show away by ill-timed remarks, Leslie was stopped short in his tracks by Andy's cold eye fixed on him.

"Now, young man," said Andy, "who are you, and what are you doing here?"

And indeed the question was only reasonable, as Leslie realized. He named himself, began some explanation of his presence, somewhat confused in that belatedly it occurred to him, when he was in the middle of it, that he was not sure how much of Amata's part in it he should tell. But apparently all this was unimportant to the *ranchero*. He brushed it aside.

"What is all this land business?" he demanded. "What is there in Folded Hills that needs investigation?"

He listened attentively and without interruption to Leslie's reply, which was succinct and straightforward, for here the young man was on the sure ground of his preparation before leaving San Francisco. Leslie was delighted to speak his piece with the authority of that preparation, for somehow it raised his stature before this man whom already he admired.

The titles to land in California, Leslie explained, under the Spanish and Mexicans were of many sorts, some of them good—most of them good. But a great many of them were vague, needed defining. And a great many more were frankly bad; grants made by the *politicos* corruptly and illegally. A few had even been found to be forged or antedated. This made so much confusion that the government had decreed that every claimant under a Spanish or Mexican title must validate his title; and for that reason every *rancho*—not merely Folded Hills—must be inspected and passed by a commission. Any grants not so confirmed became part of the public domain.

"I've heard nothing of this," said Andy. "But then," he added, "I have taken no part in affairs since the Occupation." He was thoughtful for a moment. "Why did you lie to that man?" he asked abruptly, and with a snap of sternness.

"Lie?" stammered Leslie, taken aback.

"You told him you were doing this job, that it was almost finished. That was not true. Why?"

Leslie recovered himself. He looked straight into Andy's eyes, and his own slowly crinkled in an engaging smile.

"Why did you agree with me, sir?" he asked with entire respect.

Andy stared for a moment, then laughed shortly, but with genuine appreciation. His manner changed. His long form relaxed; he stretched out his legs lazily.

"Reckon you got me there, bub," he acknowledged. His voice had resumed its lazy drawl. "I'll tell you. I followed your play because I liked your looks, and I didn't like the looks of this other feller. But I didn't know what your play was, and I don't now, and I think you'd better tell me. Don't you?"

"Yes, sir," said Leslie. "You see, sir, I was going up beyond St. Anthony of Padua to a *rancho* belonging to a Señor Constansio."

"A mite off your route here," pointed out Andy.

"Yes, sir." Leslie passed that by and hurried on. "I was waiting here when you came up. I couldn't help hearing what that man said to you. I'd seen him before, but I didn't know that he was a government agent. But I remembered what I'd heard another man say to him when they were talking about squatter troubles—something about how much land would he need for his next gang—and all of a sudden it came to me how easy it would be for him to put in a report that would make trouble or fix it so the claim, or maybe only a part of it, would be rejected, and so—don't you see how easy it would be? Especially if someone was backing him among these new settlers, and——" The words were tumbling over one another in his eagerness. Andy was watching him intently.

"Hold on"—his cool tones interrupted the torrent—"you're going too fast. You think this man, Ransom, might be playing cahoots with somebody to get a hold of my land? Is that it?" He chuckled at Leslie's assent. "Of course they'd always have to come and *git* it." His lips set tight for a moment, but instantly relaxed to amusement again. "And where do you come in?" he asked.

"Why"—Leslie was thrown off his stride—"why, I thought that maybe if we got rid of him that—that I——" He floundered. Of a sudden it was not very clear even to him. He reddened but held his ground. "It sounds pretty impudent, sir," he said stoutly, "but somebody's got to do it—that's the new law—and I thought that perhaps I could at least send in an honest report, and I don't believe this man would."

He was aware of Andy's grave scrutiny.

"I'm an old Mountain Man," said the latter after a moment, "and I like to read my sign clear. And there's two things I don't quite *sabe*. If things are like you say, why should this man come way out here, leagues from nowhere, to get him his land for his gang, as you call 'em, when there's land aplenty nearer home? That's one. And t'other is, how does it come you're so all-fired anxious to horn in on a total stranger that is nothing to you? And I've got yet to hear why you're right here so pat, two leagues off your route—ef'n you're really headed for Constansio's."

Andy clasped his hands behind his head and examined the young man before him with half-closed eyes. His tone was almost insolently challenging, yet beneath the veil of his eyelids lurked still a spark of lazy amusement.

Leslie reddened to the insolence, which seemed real enough to him. He drew himself up stiffly.

"I am sorry," he said with dignity. "I shall not trouble you further."

He turned away but found the effect of his exit somewhat marred by the fact that his horse had been taken away and he had no place to go. Likewise there lay his saddlebags and *cantinas*. He turned with what dignity he could summon to make the necessary request. The man was smiling at him.

"Don't get mad, bub," said Andy. "I was only teasing you a mite. Bless you, I know boys. I've got one, just about your age. And I know men. I ought to by now. I've seed enough of 'em and enough kinds in my time. Didn't I follow along with your game?" he reminded. "I don't doubt you for a minute. You come over here and sit down. Now tell me all about this. It's a pretty blind trail from where I am."

Reluctantly at first Leslie obeyed. But Andy's warmth was genuine, and he had turned serious.

"Now it makes sense," observed the latter with satisfaction, when he heard of Djo's encounter with Ransom. "I wondered." He looked at Leslie keenly. "So you came over here to see Djo, eh? Djo's at Monterey. He'll be back tomorrow."

Leslie hesitated, reddened.

"No, sir," he said frankly. "I didn't even know Djo lived here. I'd have come, if I had known." He stopped, reflecting swiftly on the rigid Spanish convention; reflected further that the manner of his arrival was already known. "Your daughter brought me here," he confessed. "We met over the hills yonder, about six miles."

"Amata? She brought you here?" Leslie imagined a stiffening in his host's manner. "How did that happen?"

Painfully but honestly Leslie detailed the episode. He did not spare either his ignorance or what he called his stupidity. He even told of the derringer.

"I'm new to the country," confessed Leslie stoutly. "I'm afraid I'm an awful greenhorn." This was not easy to say, in view of the Colt's revolving pistol and the sky-for-his-roof.

The *ranchero* surveyed him with approval.

"That's right, son," said he. "Don't try to be what you ain't. It can't be done. I knew all that. As for being a greenhorn"—he paused, and his keen gray eyes softened and became far away—"when I was about your age—maybe a trifle younger—I was just starting out, on foot, from home—to try my luck in the world, out West." He chuckled. "I thought I was quite a figure of a woodsman with my rifle over my shoulder and my bundle at my back. Old Dan'l Boone was nothing to me—by the way, the rifle I carried once belonged to old Dan'l. I thought I was some pumpkins. I see now I was the greenest green-horn that ever stepped. A man gets over being a greenhorn, ef'n he's a man. There's worse things . . ." His voice trailed off in rumination. "There's a passel of things happened since then. That's a long time ago." He lost himself in reverie. Leslie looked at him, fascinated by something strong and sure he could divine but could not identify. Andy looked up with a twinkle. "You'll stay and see Djo," he stated, rather than invited. "You two'll team well. He can learn you lots, and I reckon you can give him a few pointers, too. Shucks!" said Andy to Leslie's half demur. "Never mind Constansio; he'll keep. You've got a job here, ain't you?" He grinned relishingly. "I'll dig up the papers and *diseño*, and you can go at it—whatever it is." Andy's manner was of tolerant amusement. "Djo'll help you." He laid his hand on Leslie's arm. "I'd like for you to know Djo," he said persuasively, "and I'd like for Djo to know you."

Leslie warmed to the obvious approval of the *ranchero* for himself, though its reason was obscure to him. But the sincerity of the invitation was unmistakable.

"What say?" urged Andy.

"I'd like nothing better in the world!" cried Leslie. The thought of Djo struck him with another thought.

"This Ransom!" he cried.

"What about him?"

"He came to make trouble."

"Well, you headed that off—for now, anyway," said Andy comfortably. "We got rid of him."

"But he's not going to give up that easily."

"Probably not," agreed Andy. "We'll try to handle him when the time comes."

"But Djo!"

"What about Djo?"

"Aren't you afraid that Ransom will—that Ransom may——"

"Oh, Djo will take care of himself. I've l'arned him that."

"But this man is armed, and Djo——"

"Djo," said Andy emphatically, "knows this man is somewhere in the country and must be layin' to get even. That's enough. He will be armed by now, and he'll sure see him first, and don't you fret about his gettin' ambushed because Djo won't be ridin' within long range of ary ambushes. Besides," added Andy, "this Ransom didn't come up here to pick any row with just a pistol. Not yet. His arm is hurt."

"What did he come for, then?" demanded Leslie.

"I don't know: spying around, perhaps." He grinned. "Aiming to steal the *rancho,* didn't you say?" This idea continued to amuse him.

"He might have confederates with him."

"You won't be a greenhorn long," observed Andy approvingly. Nevertheless he failed to be perturbed. "We'll know, come night, as soon as the *mozas* come in," he said presently. He looked at Leslie's face and chuckled under his breath. "There's no keeping things hid in this country, son." He relented to explanation: "Down at the creek the *mozas* wash clothes all day and talk; about an equal share of each, I should judge. Every *vaquero* and *mozo* and Injun—and the dickybirds, I sometimes think—traveling about the country for any reason whatever sees to it they cross the creek where the girls are washing; and they tell all they know. And the *mozas* spread the news. And tell it back. Beats the telegraph. If anything ever happened that wasn't known from one end of the country to the other by sundown, I never heard of it. If this Ransom has a gang, we'll know and take measures according." He arose and stretched his long form.

Leslie arose with him.

"I hope I didn't get Miss Amata in any trouble," said he respectfully.

Andy stopped and looked at him.

"Trouble? What trouble?"

Leslie expounded.

"She tell you all that?" Andy seemed incredulous. He laughed suddenly with great relish. "Well, seems like the Doña Amata"—he chuckled again at the name—"is growed up all of a sudden. I can't recall anybody worrying about all that truck before. Mebbe we'd better go see if old Vicenta has sculped her!"

VI

EVIDENTLY Amata was not "sculped." Indeed, as far as Leslie could see, no one, save Amata herself, appeared to be inclined to pay any attention to the matter. The dreaded Vicenta was most amiable.

"He is the smiling one," said she.

But it was Djo, who returned next day, who, with fraternal indifference, put the young lady's romantic pretensions in their place.

"Amata!" he snorted when he heard. "That *niña pequeña!* She's always trying to make people think she's grown up!"

His attitude toward Amata's inclination to ally herself

with any of the lads' expeditions or activities was of denial or easy tolerance. Leslie suddenly saw her as a child, a charming child, but a child nevertheless. This was the private solace of his pride. But in her company somehow, he stepped warily and eyed askance, for, though she might indeed be but a child, there was something very close beneath the surface that at once attracted and made cautious the young man's spirit.

Djo was, naturally, overjoyed to find his new acquaintance at the *rancho*. This occupied his mind, so that he merely nodded when Leslie excitedly told him of Ransom's visit to the *rancho*. But Leslie noticed, in spite of this apparent indifference, that, true to Andy's prediction, Djo had arrived with a rifle across his saddle.

Naturally, Djo took Leslie in charge, and eagerly. He must do the honors, show him all there was to be seen, do with him all there was to do. This, on such a ranch, was a tremendous lot, and it was all strange and interesting to Leslie.

At first they rode: from morning to night. Leslie found himself furnished with fresh horses, new equipment, even garments more appropriate than the few his saddlebags had contained. The latter disappeared. He never saw them again. He learned of the cattle business, and the milling business, and the intricate business of the vineyards and grainfields and *milpas,* all of which fascinated him. He liked every little detail, even to the choking dust of the corrals where the branding was done, and he eagerly asked dozens of questions, generally of Djo or Andy, but failing them of anyone he met. The people of the *rancho* liked him. He was unashamed of his ignorance and his faulty Spanish. He was repeatedly trying to translate literally English idioms, or even slang phrases. The results were sometimes astounding. At first his interlocutors struggled for politeness, but finding him ready to laugh wholeheartedly with them, a good time was had by all. He was a smiling one.

And he wanted to try everything. He practiced tirelessly with the *reata*. He and Djo spent hours with the Colt's revolving pistol, banging away at a mark. Here was one thing Djo envied him. They burned so much powder and made so much noise that finally by request they moved their range down in the flat, a little farther from the house. This was an absorbing occupation. There was plenty of technique to figure out, not only as to the shooting itself, but in such minor matters as molding successful bullets. It took several trials before they were able to tap from the mold shining silverlike bullets undisturbed by shrunken metal or bubble holes: a matter of temperatures, both of the metal and of the mold itself.

Djo was already a fair shot, but Leslie at first was likely to miss the whole tree to which their mark was pegged. The weapon jumped wildly and erratically, and try as he might he could not avoid anticipating the loud black-powder *bang* of the discharge. Djo could not help him much with theory.

"You just got to get used to it," said he. "It's practice."

But Leslie's mind had an analytical quirk.

"Practice is all right," he returned, "if you know what you're practicing at."

He brooded over the elements of the situation, took them apart in his mind, had an idea.

"Look here, Djo," said he, "the pistol goes off when the hammer hits the cap. Don't it?"

"Why, sure!" agreed Djo to the self-evident.

"We've been thinking the kick throws the shot high. Let's find out."

Leslie extended the weapon and took careful aim.

"You've got no cap on," Djo pointed out.

"That's just the idea." Leslie aimed again and pulled the trigger. "Just as I thought!" he cried with mingled triumph and chagrin. "The muzzle jerked up a foot!

Don't you see? If we can't hold the muzzle where we aim until the bullet's gone, we aren't going to hit anything. The bullet's going just exactly where the muzzle points. We got to keep aiming *after* we pull the trigger. Here; try it!"

Djo tried it, tried it again and again.

"Doggone!" he muttered. "I flinched off every time!"

"I don't believe," said Leslie, "that the kick has anything to do with it!"

This was too radical for immediate acceptance.

The actual shooting ceased. The two lads took turn snapping the empty pistol. Even after the involuntary flinching from the explosion had been eliminated from their minds, they found the greatest difficulty in keeping the sights aligned on the mark after the fall and jar of the hammer. Both had steady hands and nerves and keen eyesight. There was no difficulty in taking good aim and holding it *until* the trigger was pulled. Why was that?

"Practice," said Djo; but Leslie worried and experimented until he had, empirically, stumbled on another great principle.

"Don't grip it tight. Hold it loose," he said. "The looser you hold it in your hand, the better you can hold it on. Try it."

Djo tried it.

"That's right," he acknowledged. "But," he objected, "that's all right for an empty gun, but if you're going actually to shoot it you've got to hold it tight or it'll kick all over the place."

"Let's see," said Leslie. He loaded and capped the weapon. "Stand back," he advised Djo. "This thing may jump out of my hand and bite you. I'm going to let it just *lay* in my hand. Let's see how far off she can kick."

He fired. The pistol leaped, all but wrenching itself from Leslie's loosened hand. But the bullet, for the first time, hit squarely in the small blaze they were using as a mark. Djo and Leslie looked at one another ecstatically. They solemnly shook hands.

"We've got it by the tail," said Djo.

After which, of course, a measure of disillusion. Conquests are not made as easily as all that. The gap between even the most perfect theory and performance cannot be leaped. It must be bridged. But only a measure. There was now something definite to be worked upon.

Andy, passing, sometimes dismounted and squatted on his heels apart, listening. He was much amused and more than a little interested. Appealed to, in the early stages, for instruction, he was unable to contribute much. "You've got to squeeze the trigger" was all he could tell them. On request he fired a few rounds to show them. There was not much to see, except that his large strong hand looked to be as steady as a vise, and the bullets grouped discouragingly in or close to the blaze on the tree. "You just shoot," said he vaguely. He honestly did not know how he did it, nor appreciate the long years that lay back of his coördinations. He examined the bullet holes disparagingly. "Those things can't shoot close, like a good rifle," said he. "They really ain't much good. Unless you l'arn to shoot 'em fast. That's what I practice at, myself." He buckled on the holster. "Look here," said he. He snatched out the weapon and fired, in one coördinated motion of shoulder, arm, hand, and thumb. The bullet hit the tree a foot or so from the blaze. "That's close enough for what these things are good for. You hunch your shoulder forward," he explained.

"But you've got to learn to hit *something* slow before you can hit anything fast," submitted Leslie respectfully.

"That's right, I reckon," admitted Andy.

That was his only demonstration. He sat apart on his heels and listened, while his beautiful horse stood above him champing the rollers of its bit, its ears flicking and its nostrils expanding to an inaudible snort at each discharge, disliking the noise intensely, but too well trained to expostulate openly.

Andy made no comments, but to Carmel he said later:

"*Querida,* that boy has a good head on his shoulders. He's taught me a lot I don't know about shooting."

Carmel turned on him her beautiful eyes.

"You, *mi almo?* This one has taught *you* to shoot!"

"Not *how* to shoot; *why* I shoot," corrected Andy. He explained. "He figured all that out himself. He's going to do Djo a lot of good. I'm glad he came along. We must try to keep him."

2

Amata, snubbed once or twice by Djo, left the two young men quite strictly to themselves. She caused Leslie to understand that their absorption in noisy and dusty activities did not appeal to her. She busied herself about the *casa* or rode abroad, either alone or with her father or an old hard-bitten *vaquero* called Panchito. Her cool and detached, not to say amused, attitude rather shook Leslie's impression of her childishness. He began to regret his hasty adoption of Djo's point of view. It might have been pleasant to have gone along on some of these rides, but

Djo was always on hand with some fresh proposal, and he a little deprecated Djo's opinion. Once Amata took a dig at Djo.

"You're just showing off to him," she said.

Djo, stung, repelled this insinuation indignantly.

"I am not so!" he cried. "It's just that he's so green about everything. But he learns fast," he added loyally. He stared at Amata, perplexed, seeing her with new eyes.

The evenings, shortened by early bedtime, were spent in the great hallway of the *casa*. The Doña Carmel sewed or embroidered. Andy smoked his pipe. Amata usually sat still as a mouse by her mother's side, engaged in her own handiwork. There was a variety of small talk, mostly to do with the affairs of the *rancho,* and occasionally music of singing to the guitar. The framework was simple to the point of dullness, yet it was not dull somehow. One evening, unexpectedly, Amata took the lead. She began to question Leslie, to draw him out as to the cities of the East: his own home, the affairs of the larger world from which he had come. Leslie answered readily enough, but diffidently. He had not thought such humdrum matters could possibly interest people living in the very heart of romance. He was not yet experienced enough to realize that romance is over the hill.

"Why, I came from Pennsylvania as a lad!" cried Andy when this fact came out. His interest kindled. He began, in his turn, to ask questions. Amata fell silent, a faint satisfied smile on her lips. Carmel looked at her covertly, with speculation. However, Amata was merely putting Djo in his place.

At the end of a wholly delightful week, however, Leslie's conscience aroused. He importuned Andy until the latter, half amused, half annoyed, at last consented to rummage for the papers and the *diseño* that represented his title to Folded Hills.

"I'm not even sure I got one," he grumbled. "Señor Casteñares made 'em out. That was years ago. I didn't pay much attention. I was too busy to go out with him. I think Panchito was with him. I'll ask Panchito. There were papers all right: I remember them, but I'm not sure Casteñares didn't take 'em with him to Monterey. I remember! It was time of the rodeo, and we had a passel of folks here for the *fiesta!* Don't they record these things?"

"Yes," said Leslie. "We could get copies. I have copies of the Constansio ranch—where I was going, you know. But if you had them——"

"I'll ask Mrs. Burnett," said Andy, giving it up.

Carmel promptly produced the required documents.

Andy passed them over, apparently without curiosity as to what was to be done with them, or interest.

3

Leslie and Djo, and later Panchito, rode the *rancho* for several days, trying to identify landmarks, to establish the boundaries. It was impossible to do so with any accuracy. "A white-oak tree," "a curious rock," "a mound of earth." Many of them, apparently destroyed or disappeared. Others existing in bewildering duplication. Distances and compass directions sometimes flatly contradictory. The whole thing was a mess: a jumble. Leslie could make no head or tail of it. Panchito, though he had been present, was not of much help. Except that he could, under close questioning, give Leslie some idea of how this extraordinary hodgepodge had been accomplished. The whole survey had been done on horseback, generally at a lope.

"But how could measurements be taken?" cried Leslie.

By a *reata*. A horseman dropped one end and paid it out until he reached the other. At full gallop? But of course; how else? And how about while the rider was recovering and recoiling the *reata?* Oh, allowance was made for that. But how? By guess? But surely; how else?

Stampede

Leslie looked about him in despair. He reapplied himself to the terms of the grant. It was an impressive document, on parchment, with a great seal and the signature of the governor, Figueroa, in a fine flourish. It read well and fluently. "South three hundred and fifty *estradas* to a large live-oak tree, thence a hundred and twenty-five *estradas* to a white oak riven by the wind," and so on, from one point to another. It was all very clear, except for one thing: there was rarely by any chance a live oak or a white oak or a curious rock or whatever within any reasonable distance of where it ought to be. The indications—or rather those Leslie guessed at as being the nearest to description—led them on and on until even Djo stopped, bewildered.

"But this is not the boundary of Folded Hills!" he cried. "Folded Hills extends way over the hills yonder!"

"Let's go back and try again," said Leslie. In spite of the fact that he seemed the volatile, and Djo the steadfast, character, it was Leslie who stuck to the task obstinately long after Djo's patience was exhausted. But Djo did not as yet take the matter very seriously. Leslie's mind had been educated to a more formal politic. He was appalled.

The day was strong with the dry heat of interior California that smells hot and tastes hot in the nostrils, but in which is no prostration. They drew up finally in the shade of a wide live oak and dismounted for a little, while Panchito squatted apart, holding the horses. Djo was chuckling at their discomfiture.

"Well, are you licked, old stick-to-it?" he asked affectionately.

Leslie had difficulty making him see the gravity of the situation, or rather its grave possibilities. As the matter stood right now, it would be entirely possible for any stranger to file on at least the outlying acres of Folded Hills, with a very fair possibility that he would, in fact, be taking up legally public land. As a usual thing, legal remedying of defective titles was so long drawn out and involved and expensive that, when the smoke had cleared away, it was likely that nothing remained. Leslie was eloquent with examples; the result of his week's investigation. Few of these large landholders had any ready money with which to pay lawyers or taxes or the expense of defense. To raise such funds they had often to sell part of the land. Land whose title was clouded fetched only a fraction of its real value, for only speculators would buy it—or the sharper lawyers, who were on the inside. If the case was decided in the landowner's favor, it was almost invariably appealed to the higher local court, thence to

Washington. There was no end to it. More and more fees and costs. The necessity of raising more money. Generally the lawyers were willing to take their fees, immense fees, in land and cattle; and so gradually they and their clients changed places, and the lawyers became the *hacendados*. That's the way it had happened, was happening about the Bay.

"We don't want your father to get into that kind of a mess," said Leslie.

"I should say not!" cried Djo.

All that was bad enough, but there was the further matter of squatters: such as had overwhelmed Don Luis Peralta. They had no legal standing whatever, of course, but they had legal backing. At first merely a scattering of the truculent who took land defiantly because they wanted it, they had become powerful. Leslie tried to impress on the skeptical Djo how this could be. The squatters were organized. They elected senators, judges, court officials, land officials. At times they even opposed legal ejectment with arms.

"You heard what Ransom said about the cannon over at Peralta's," said Leslie.

The slightest rumor that the title of any land might prove shaky attracted a swarm of these people. Many had no intention of trying to hold their claims. They established themselves in the hope of selling out cheap to some of the land-hungry on their way across the plains.

To Djo most of this did not at first seem credible. He had to end by believing, for Leslie's knowledge was exact and detailed and fortified with examples.

"I'd heard something of these troubles, but I had no idea," said Djo. He ended by catching Leslie's disquiet. Vallejo himself, it seemed, was deeply involved. What was there to do?

"Get the title straight," said Leslie promptly. "That's why we've got to trace out this boundary if we can. So I can make a good report. If I can't report everything in order, don't you see what will happen? As soon as it got out, they'd be down here like a swarm of locusts."

"Who?"

"The squatters. The least little rumor that the title of any land might turn out to be shaky and they come arunning. Those are mostly the sort that squat and hang on long enough to sell out to someone really looking for a farm. They sell out cheap and move on. They only try it where the title is in doubt. The real squatters settle down anywhere, regardless."

"How do you know so much about all this?" Djo

looked at him with an admiration that brought to Leslie's spirit a comforting glow. Leslie had been, at Folded Hills, the humble greenhorn.

"Part of my job," said he.

Of course Folded Hills was a long distance back, still . . .

"Let's go back to the *mojonera* and start over again," said Djo, rising.

They mounted and rode back to the *mojonera*, the official starting point of Casteñares' original "survey." It was clearly identifiable, "a monument of rounded stones in which is planted a wooden cross." The wooden cross had long since disintegrated, but the pile of stones was still there. But the fresh start gave no better result. The original inaccuracies of measurement and direction would probably have been sufficient. But additionally—and neither Djo nor Leslie could know that—the very location of the *mojonera* was fictitious. It was supposed to abut a corner of El Rancho Soledad. But Señor Casteñares had been unable to find monuments of the latter. He did not look long.

"Ah, well," he had said comfortably, "it is undoubtedly somewhere in this valley," and had wasted no more time in the matter, but had built himself a new one.

Djo drew rein and looked hopelessly at his friend.

"The thing to do," said Leslie with decision, "is to get the boundaries properly surveyed and marked—in accordance with this." He brushed the parchment grant with the flat of his hand. "Then one would fit with the other, anyway."

"Why, of course." Djo was obviously relieved. He appeared to think this solved the whole situation and looked at his friend with admiration. "Who does it? You?"

"I?" Leslie laughed.

"Well, you're a land officer, aren't you?"

"That's the point. I'm a land officer, and I mustn't know anything is wrong here until it's all right. I've got to report what I find. There are probably regular surveyors to be had at Monterey. But it ought to be done right away. I'll have to make my report, you know." He caught a queer look in Djo's eyes. "I'm under oath, you know," said he.

Djo nodded soberly. He was deeply impressed.

"Let's go back to the *casa* and talk to my father," said he.

4

They remounted and jogged slowly cross country in the direction of the *casa*. This was now latter April, the

Stampede

gorgeous turn of the year. The wild flowers lay in brilliant blankets of orange and yellow and blue flung over the hills, whose green was blurring toward an imminent ripeness. The air was an infusion of sunlight and sun warmth that held all things in solution, so that bird liltings and calls, hot perfumes, blue-toned shadows, and the harlequin colors of the hills were by it all blended into one impression of consciousness. It was good to be alive and to breathe deep.

Atop the first rise of the foothills they drew rein and looked back over the broad flat of the valley. Between its confining ramparts it flowed like a river to lose itself in a brown mist of distance, beyond which was the sea. On its bosom floated tiny the details of its identity. There were the dabs of green that were the scattered oaks, and the strips of green that were the cottonwoods and sycamores of the river, and a splash of white so small that almost it must be guessed, and that must be the Mission of Nuestra Señora de la Soledad.

Djo's eyes narrowed to a focus. He touched Leslie's arm. From behind the shoulder of a hill below them appeared a horseman. He was riding at a foot pace and peering about him closely as though in search of something, so closely that he did not look up to see the three on the sky line above him. Djo, his eyes dancing, signaled caution to his companions and slowly backed his horse into the concealment of the chaparral. The others imitated him. Leslie looked his inquiry, but Djo paid him no attention. From the screen of the brush they watched the man below them.

The latter zigzagged, almost as though at random, spying his immediate surroundings, turning often in his saddle to look back. When he came to the pile of stones, the *mojonera,* he stopped his horse. Djo at last turned to Leslie.

"Do you know who it is?" he asked excitedly in a low voice. "It's Ransom!"

"Ransom!" repeated Leslie, dumfounded. "Are you sure? I couldn't make out at that distance."

"It's Ransom," repeated Djo emphatically, "and you know what I think? He's following us: that's just where we came from."

"Gosh!" cried Leslie. "What'll we do?"

The boys looked at one another. For a time they had carried with them on their excursions the Colt's revolving pistol, but its oppressive weight had outlasted its romance. They were unarmed. Djo spoke rapidly to Panchito in Spanish.

Stampede

"We could ride him down with our *reatas*," said he. "I don't believe he could hit us with a pistol."

But Leslie's very inexperience gave him the cooler, or perhaps the more cautious, head.

"He has a rifle—under his leg," he pointed out, "and, anyway, what right have we got to attack him without knowing for sure that he *is* after us?"

Djo looked at him with amazed scorn.

"What else is he hanging around here for?" he wanted to know.

Nevertheless Leslie clung to his point. It was finally agreed that they should arm themselves at the *casa*, return, call upon Ransom for an accounting of his presence at Folded Hills.

"Though we really don't know if it *is* Folded Hills," Leslie reminded with a flash of humor.

Panchito would stay here.

"You will see in which direction this one goes," Djo instructed him. "But he must not know you watch him. And wait here until we return. If he follows our tracks up the hill, then slip away and ride to let us know. Understand?"

"Have no fear, *patroncito*," said Panchito comfortably.

The two dropped over the brow of the hill and raced

away. They returned within the hour, armed with the derringer, the revolving pistol, and a rifle.

"He must be still in the valley—otherwise Panchito would have met us," panted Djo. "What can he be doing there?"

"Lying in wait for us," hazarded Leslie. "We've been riding there a lot lately looking for the boundary. He saw it by our tracks."

Djo nodded. They slackened down, crept forward to where they had left Panchito. Panchito was still there, sprawled out at ease, smoking a cigarette.

"He has ridden away, down the valley," said Panchito. "In the direction of Soledad."

"Come on!" said Djo.

The three followed after Ransom. To Leslie it was very interesting, for immediately the flat country was reached, Djo led them aside, so they followed, not on Ransom's direct trail, but off the flank. Every so often they stopped, and either Djo or Panchito rode at right angles to cut the tracks and redetermine their direction. Soon it became evident that the man was angling toward the Camino Real, the regular route north and south. Once he had reached this, he pursued his journey methodically. He passed Soledad. He continued on toward the west. Djo drew rein.

"There's no sense going farther," said he. "It's getting late. I can't make it out. What is he doing, Panchito?" he asked in Spanish.

"He is going away," replied the *vaquero*.

Djo laughed vexedly. "Evidently. But why? Where did he come from? Has he been around here all the time since he visited the *rancho?* If so, where's he been staying? What is he after?"

"I suppose he wants to get even with you—with us," suggested Leslie.

"Then why hasn't he? He must have had chances—for ambush! Well"—Djo set his jaw grimly—"he won't have any more!"

He turned his horse, shaking his head, puzzled.

"Well, come on!" He struck spurs to his horse. "Let's get home. It'll be dark——"

VII

THEY took Andy apart after the evening meal. He listened, questioning them sharply as to a detail now and again.

"Why should he want to bother Leslie?" He caught up that point.

"Because Leslie gave me his pistol that time we had our little mix-up," said Djo.

"You didn't tell me about that," Andy accused Leslie.

"It wasn't anything," the latter disclaimed.

Andy grunted. His eye was kind.

"I don't know," he said when the story was finished,

"why he didn't take a pot shot: he must have had plenty chances. Nothing to go on. You think he's gone?"

"We followed him beyond Soledad, and he was still going," said Djo.

"Well, we'll make sure." He stepped to the door and issued an order. To Panchito he said, "Send one of the Indians—Ramirex—to follow the way this man has gone and see that he has not doubled back. He may have seen you on the hill and is doing this to fool you," he told the two young men. Having given this command, he apparently dismissed the whole matter from his mind. Nor was he particularly impressed by what Leslie had to say of the boundary situation. He nodded gravely to the young man's arguments.

"That's very interesting," he said. "I had no idea things were quite so bad. I'm obleeged to you, Leslie. First chance I get I'll have someone come up from Monterey to make a survey." But he could not promise to do so immediately. "I reckon I'd have to go myself," said he. "Since Tom Larkin moved to San Francisco, I wouldn't know who to write a letter to. And we're going to be busy now with the spring rodeo."

The reasons for haste did not impress him.

"Nobody's going to bother us way out here," said he.

"Be reasonable. What those fellers want is farm claims, and there are thousands of acres to squabble over a sight nearer the cities than we are here. Now why," said Andy, "should anybody come this far to squat on land when there's aplenty nearer home?"

It was pointed out to him that Leslie's official position required him to make a report which, once it was in, would place on file for all time irregularities that might make trouble. Andy appeared to consider this seriously, though the mention of the official position brought a twinkle to his eye.

"Better postpone it till after the rodeo anyway," he suggested. "You've never seen a rodeo. You'll like it. Only means a week or so. And then why can't you go up to Constansio's and do your work there; and by the time you get that done I'll have things straightened out here. You supposed to get back to San Francisco any particular time?"

That seemed to be a sound idea. Andy went on about his preparations for the rodeo. Though he tried to conceal the fact, he did not take the matter seriously. Undoubtedly the stories Leslie had to tell were true, at least in part. But Andy knew that many of the alleged Spanish grants were indeed fraudulent, dished out corruptly and illegally by some of the later Mexican governors in a scramble to get something for themselves before the collapse. Larkin had told him something of that. Some pieces of land were covered, it was said, by five different grants! But Folded Hills was an old establishment; it came direct from Figueroa. Andy could not believe that any small technicalities could affect him. And as a loyal American he could not conceive that any real injustice would be long tolerated.

2

The Indian reported that Ransom had kept on going, had not doubled back.

"Well, I can't figure him," said Andy, perplexed. However, he had no time to waste on mere theory. "Keep your eyes skinned, Djo, case he comes back," and made no further reference to the episode.

Nor did it long linger in Leslie's thoughts except as something vague over the horizon of the future, to be taken up later, like this land-inspection business. The immediate present was full, gorgeously full, bewilderingly full.

Leslie at times felt his flesh surreptitiously to be sure he was really awake and present. The thing was unbelievably stage-set, romantic, picturesque. The *casa* overflowed with people, come in from the neighboring *ranchos* for the occasion, all sorts of people, young and old, of both sexes. Most of them dressed in what, to Leslie, was an extreme of fancy-dress costume. They were dark and handsome and lighthearted, and they took the young stranger to their hearts with a touching spontaneity. The days brimmed full with doings, from morning starlight, when the men rode forth in the dusk on the business of the cattle, until all hours of the night, when the last guitar muted. The serious work of the year was forward and was efficiently performed, but somehow it was so intermingled with picnic and games and dance and feast and a sly gallant love-making that it was tossed off as a heady draught of pleasure. When the last guest had departed, Leslie drew a deep breath and looked about him as though awakening from a dream. Somehow a long period of time seemed to have elapsed, though the rodeo had actually lasted but a week. And the placidity of life seemed only slowly to reëstablish itself, to resume its accustomed routine.

So real was this impression of lapse of time that Leslie was unreasonably conscience-stricken over his own dawdling. After all, he told himself, he was a government official, and he had raised his hand and sworn an oath to be honest and diligent about the government's affairs, and he supposed he was drawing some sort of a salary. Or was he? Leslie stopped short, laughed at himself. This was the first time that question had occurred to him. At any rate, he had no excuse to stay on at Folded Hills. At the rodeo he had met Señor Constansio, a very dignified white-bearded old fellow, who had assured Leslie he would be more than welcome at Alisal, but who had the greatest difficulty in comprehending his errand there. However, if Don Andreo approved, it was all right. *A rividerse, señor.* Andy laughed.

"I doubt if you'll find Alisal much better marked than Folded Hills," said he. "Or any other of the *ranchos*, as far as that goes. I was talking to Ramon about it—Ramon Rivera—you know, the one who talks English. He's Mrs. Burnett's brother. He has a *rancho* over Jolon way. We thought it might be a good idea, once we get us that surveyor from Monterey, to have him go over all the *ranchos* hereabouts and straighten 'em all out. There's only a half a dozen or so."

Leslie thought this an excellent idea and said so. He had no specific instructions, except as to the Constansio *rancho*, but he saw no reason why he should not extend his operations. That would take some time. He saw himself much at Folded Hills. Perhaps it would be possible to make his headquarters at Folded Hills. Leslie's ideas of Californian distances were still crude. He felt a great relief when his departure was thus postponed. He strongly did not want to leave Folded Hills. He liked it. He liked the life. He liked Djo. He increasingly admired Andy, in whom he had but lately discovered a veritable mine—if cautiously worked—of the most astounding adventure stories. Leslie had had no idea that his host had been an Indian fighter! He liked the Doña Carmel and her soft beautiful eyes, and her dark hair, and her comforting air of wise understanding, and her heartening fashion of treating him as a grown man of dependence. He liked Amata, at whom he looked with fresh attention now that he was so soon to depart. He even tried to make up for his absorption in Djo and men's activities by asking her to ride with him and was promptly snubbed for his pains. But Djo was wrong about one thing. She was no child, now that he took a good look at her. She was quite grown up, or would be in a year or so.

There was no reason why Leslie should not have accompanied the Constansio outfit when it returned to its *rancho*. However, he was easily persuaded to delay a day or two in order to observe and perhaps take a small part in the *matanza* that must follow the rodeo. Andy sent a messenger with a letter to Monterey, for he learned that an old friend, Jacob Leese, had moved into Larkin's house there, and Leese would get him a surveyor. Leslie took the opportunity to send out a letter which must eventually reach his uncle. It was a rather rhapsodic mixture of business and ecstasy. Its purport was to convey for approval this new idea of covering all the *ranchos;* its burden was what a perfectly tremendous time he was having. Leslie piled on the local color. Indeed he neglected to mention his present host as other than Don Andreo. There was much more atmosphere to that than plain Andy Burnett, and how could he know the difference the mention of that name might have made?

Somehow the dispatch of this document impressed Leslie's subconscious as something accomplished, so he felt justified in yielding to persuasion and accompanying Andy and Djo on an excursion through the low easterly mountains and hills toward the great Valley. This was a pleasure excursion, Mountain-Man fashion, with a single pack horse for the three and no *vaqueros*. Leslie saw elk and antelope and many deer and several of the huge, lumbering grizzly bears that stopped and stood on their hind legs, their forepaws hanging ludicrously, and wrinkled their noses in olfactory inquiry, but looked drolly good-humored. Leslie was much excited over these animals and was disappointed to find that none of them were to be killed, for he had never shot any big game. He thought he concealed this chagrin, but Andy drew Djo one side.

"Take him out and let him git him a deer," said he. "Pick you a yearlin' buck or a barren doe. We can use the meat."

So after a number of mortifying failures, which Djo comfortingly took in his stride, Leslie triumphantly potted his first deer.

That night's camp was made in a stream bottom where the last of the hills broke into the great Valley of the Joaquin. Leslie had never been more happy in his life. The air was tepid; the sky hung low with stars. The velvet of night covered the earth. The firelight illumined the sycamore over their heads with weird upward-flung shadows. The three men sat cross-legged, each with a rib of venison in his hand. Other ribs, roasting, leaned toward the flames, and their juices fell softly hissing in the embers. Altogether to Leslie a completely satisfactory picture. He reveled inwardly at being a part of it.

Suddenly Andy threw up his head in the attitude of listening.

Stampede   133

"Someone coming," he said under his breath.

Leslie could hear nothing at all, but he knew by Djo's expression that he, too, had caught the indication. Leslie started to speak but was warned to silence.

"Don't know who that can be this time of night," muttered Andy.

As though by common consent he and Djo seized their rifles and rose swiftly to their feet. Obeying a signal, Leslie followed. The three glided into the darkness beyond the firelight and lay flat.

"No hostile Injuns this side of the Valley, far as I know," whispered Andy, "but no use to take a chance."

Leslie's heart beat with a delirious excitement. He thrilled from head to foot. Indians!

Now even he could hear the sounds of an approaching horse.

"He's alone," said Andy, sitting up and stretching his arms. "Still, we'll just bide here and see what he looks like."

After a moment Panchito rode into the firelight and stopped, looking about him.

"Señor!" he called. "Don Andreo!" His eyes narrowed as the others moved in the darkness. "Señor." He bent from his saddle to converse rapidly in Andy's ear. Andy turned to the young men. His face had a queer expression, but his eyes were steady and undisturbed.

"Ransom's back," said he, "and he's brought a passel of people with him."

VIII

IN THE precision and swiftness of the next few minutes nothing more was said and explained. Panchito brought in the horses, shifted his saddle to the back of the animal that had been used for packing, turned loose the one he had ridden. Andy and Djo deftly bundled the items of the simple camp equipment and lashed it in the branches of the tree. They worked silently and intently. Within the five minutes they were in the saddle and away.

Leslie had never ridden at speed, in the dark, over a rough country. Uncontrolledly his mind and his nerves shrank back from this headlong plunge into the unseen;

his body was tense with muscles braced against a fall. He tried, but in vain, to emulate the free and apparently careless swing of his companions in their saddles. Mentally he could manage it, for brief periods; but his instincts were stronger. Once Andy spoke to him.

"Slack your reins; give him his head," said he, "but keep ready to pick him up if he stumbles."

By the grace of heaven, as Leslie thought, the beast did not stumble, for he had not the vaguest idea of how he was to pick him up if he did. At the end of a half-hour or so Andy drew rein. They proceeded for a while at a foot pace to recover the horses. Not until then did Leslie learn the whole of Panchito's tidings.

These people, according to Panchito, had made camp down the valley, at the end of the grainfield, below the *milpas*. He had not seen them, but it was reported that they numbered a half hundred or so. They had come in horse-drawn wagons. There were women. Beyond that he knew nothing. He had come away promptly in search of the *patrón*. The señora had dispatched him at once.

And Ransom?

It was Ransom who had come to the *casa,* alone. He had demanded to see Don Andreo. When he had learned that Don Andreo was absent, he had departed, saying that he would await his return. Thus said the Doña Carmel; he, Panchito, had seen none of this. The Doña Carmel was not alarmed; the man had been polite, had made no demands. Andy shook his head, doubtful, for his mind ran on war parties, and on the plains war parties do not bring women and children. It was Leslie who guessed the clue, but then Leslie had recollection of a certain overheard conversation, and Andy had not. Diffidently he spoke up, making his suggestion.

"This doctor on the stagecoach," he said. "You remember, Djo. He asked this Ransom how many there were in his gang, how much land he could use, and said something about if he found anything good to let him know; he might turn farmer himself. And, yes, I'm beginning to remember —before that Ransom had made some sort of brag about having something to do with the Peralta land. 'I sort of got the boys settled.' That's it. Remember?"

Andy was listening attentively.

"Do you know what I think?" Leslie was in the uplift of a gorgeous inspiration. "I don't believe this Ransom is a government man at all! I'd bet he's some kind of a lawyer, or agent, or whatever you call it, and he goes around looking up shaky titles and bringing people to take them up, and—— These people with him; they are squatters, and he's brought them here, and that's what he's been doing hanging around here; and——"

"Slow up, bub; slow up!" Andy's drawl had its underlilt of amusement, but its real tone was serious. He pondered for a moment, then slapped his thigh smartly with the flat of his hand. "That's it. It fits. He's no friend of ours!"

"What'll you do?" cried Leslie.

"How do I know till we git there?" said Andy. He leaned from his saddle to tap Leslie's shoulder. "You've got a head on you, son." He touched spurs to his horse. The little cavalcade again dashed forward. But for some time Leslie forgot to sit taut against catastrophe, but rode relaxed in the glow of the *ranchero's* approbation.

2

They arrived at Folded Hills in the gray of the first dawn, their horses slowed by the beginnings of fatigue, but still with their tails out, for these consummate horsemen had known how to conserve their energies for a notable journey. All the people of the *rancho* were gathered about and near the *casa,* men, women, and children. They crowded around the riders with many cries and exclamations. In the light of the fire someone had built beneath the live oak and a few fat-pine torches, their faces showed lighted with excitement. Some of the women were weeping dramatically, their hair unbound. Andy quieted them with a gesture.

"What has been done? Have these *e'tranjeros* attempted any harm?" he demanded.

A dozen voices answered. He quieted them, indicated one. No, it seemed, the intruders had stayed at the lower end of the valley. They had occupied themselves in mysterious business of their own, wandering by twos and threes over the flats and the lower hills. None had ventured toward the *casa* save one, who had inquired if the *patrón* had yet returned, but who had retired after receiving his answer.

"Very well"—Andy raised his voice—"return yourselves to your homes and go to sleep. Go, I tell you! There is too much noise here; you disturb the señora's rest."

He dismounted and, without looking back, strode into the house. Djo and Leslie followed.

In the *sala*, fully dressed, sat Carmel and Amata. Andy kissed them. They looked at him expectantly.

"Come," said Andy, "we are all weary. Let us get some rest."

"Rest"—Carmel shuddered—"with those *ladrónes* at our door? What shall we do?"

"Why, that," said Andy comfortably, "we shall determine in the morning." He shifted to English, including Djo and Leslie in his next remark. "Never decide anything when you're tired, less'n you have to. Vicenta will tell you: 'When you're tired every flea is an elephant.'" He made the quotation in Spanish. "Thing to do now is to go to bed and get us some sleep."

"Sleep!" cried Carmel. "I couldn't sleep!"

"Well, I could," said Andy, "and so, I reckon, could these boys. We've come quite a ways." He laid his arm across Leslie's shoulder. "And Leslie, here, has come twice as far because he's half as used to it!" He laughed at the quaintness of his conceit. "He's all right," said Andy to nobody in particular. "He came right along without a squawk."

Leslie flushed, half with embarrassment, half with pleasure. He had not known that Andy could have appreciated his involuntary nervousness. He caught Amata's eyes fixed gravely upon him, but whether with scorn or approval he could not for the life of him guess.

3

In spite of his conviction that he was too excited to sleep, Leslie dropped off promptly enough once his head had touched the pillow. Indeed he would probably have slept until noon had he not been awakened by a persistent shaking of his shoulder. He opened his eyes drowsily. Diego, one of the housemen, stood at his bedside, a tray with chocolate in his hands, showing all his teeth in a smile.

"The *patrón* sends his good morning," said he, "and would request your presence as soon as your excellency shall be pleased to dress."

"What time is it, Diego?"

"Midmorning, señor."

Ashamed of his laziness, Leslie threw aside the bedclothes. "Tell Señor Burnett I shall be there soon. Is there any news of the strangers?"

"*Nada, nada, señor.*" Diego spread wide his hands. "Now that the *patrón* is here," he added comfortably, "all will be well."

Leslie swallowed his chocolate, dressed hastily. After a moment's hesitation he resisted the temptation to buckle on the Colt's revolving pistol. Examining the reason for this, he discovered it to be based on Amata's cool scorn which had lately made him a little shy of what his host called "foofaraw." So defiantly he did buckle it on and set out.

Leslie found nobody in the hall of the *casa*. Outside the door were the Doña Carmel, Djo, and Amata. They greeted him, exchanging with him news of the night's rest, brief speculation.

"Don Andreo comes presently," said Carmel.

Leslie noticed two saddled horses awaiting in charge of Panchito, who was afoot. One of them was a beautiful creature he had not seen before, a "silver horse," a *palomino*, of creamy buckskin color with silver-white mane and tail which had been water-braided so that they rippled in waves. The animal bore a saddle which, to Leslie, was likewise strange: an elaborate affair of carved leather ornamented with silver and colored embroidery, the stirrups hooded with leather in long points that all but touched the ground. Djo caught Leslie's glance of admiration.

"It is Lucero," he said of the horse. "He is very old. He carried *mi padre* and *mi madre* when they were married, so they say. He must be twenty-five years old."

"He does not look it," said Leslie in admiration. Lu-

Stampede 143

cero's head was high, his small fine ears slanted in dainty but alert virtue, his velvet nostrils wide, his eyes fixed in haughty pride on something far away and invisible.

"He is proud that he is ridden," said Carmel simply. "That do not happen so often now. Only for ceremony."

The door opened and closed behind them. Andy appeared.

"*Querido!*" gasped Carmel. Leslie stared with all his eyes.

From the top of his head to the tip of his toes the *ranchero* was transformed. Gone were the drab and utilitarian garments to which Leslie was accustomed. Only the wide flat hat was the same, and to that had been added a wide ribbon, with a rosette, that passed under the chin. The upper part of his body was clad in a short jacket heavily laced with silver that reached hardly to the waist and failed by several inches to meet in front. Beneath it was a loose white shirt of fine linen and a wide red sash that encircled closely the waist and hips. Below Andy wore *calzoneras* of velvet—the pantaloons slashed down the side—but over them he had drawn *botas* of soft particolored leather that would reach to the middle of the thigh. However, they had been doubled over until they came to just below the knee, where they were held by garters. They were soled with rawhide, which had been led over to cover the toes and heels with the purpose of protecting the former against the stirrup hood and to support the huge spurs on the latter. One of the garters carried a knife in a sheath. Otherwise, as far as could be seen, Andy was unarmed.

"*Querido!*" repeated Carmel, but now less on a note of surprise than of pleasure. Leslie could not help but share her evident admiration, for undoubtedly the *ranchero*, with his tall spare body and the darkly handsome gravity of his face, made a fine figure of a man. Andy flashed the briefest grin in appreciation of their surprise.

"I got this place as a *californio*," said he with a certain grimness.

Carmel's brows drew together, but Leslie's ardent spirit caught the half explanation and glowed in response. He looked toward Djo. Djo, too, understood. And as a *californio* Andy intended to hold it, or not at all.

Andy swung into the saddle of the *palomino*, who pricked forward his ears, but otherwise made no motion. Djo stepped forward as a matter of course to mount the other horse.

"Not you," said Andy, "Leslie." Djo stopped in dumfounded surprise, unable to believe his ears. "I want you to stay with your mother and sister—and the *casa*," Andy explained. "Leslie is a government officer. I want an official witness."

His tone was curt and businesslike. He caught Carmel's unspoken alarm. "There'll be no trouble," he assured her, "not now. Leslie and I are just going scouting. I wouldn't take him with me if there was going to be any trouble." He noticed the Colt's revolving pistol. "Take that thing off," he ordered. "Give it to Djo. We're not on the warpath—yet."

Leslie obeyed, acutely conscious of Amata's silent scrutiny. Her face was unreadable. She had not uttered a word. But he sensed a faint underlying feminine triumph of some kind that had no reason. He scrambled into his saddle rather more hastily than he had meant to do, and the horse shied sideways and all but eluded his swing into the saddle. He did not hear what else was said before the *ranchero* turned his horse down the hill. He was too angry, not so much with that solemn-eyed little brat of a child as with himself for being bothered by what such an insect thought. Or what he thought she thought; she never said anything, come to think of it.

4

"We are going," said Andy when Leslie had caught up and drawn alongside, "to find out what this is all about. So you let me do the talking. You keep your ears open. Understand?" He spoke not unkindly, but with a certain deadly directness that silenced Leslie, except for his assent. They rode down the hill. Leslie's heart beat strongly; he fidgeted in the saddle; he hoped his hands did not tremble, nor his voice. He was not frightened, but tremendously excited, and he had no outlet. What would happen in the next hour? What sort of people were these into whose camp they were riding so confidently? What would be their own reception? What did Andy intend? What if these people—if Ransom—turned ugly, and they unarmed? He glanced sidewise with envy of his companion's calm and steady assurance. Apparently Andy had not a nerve in his body. The *palomino* stepped daintily in pride, his small ears swinging rhythmically to his pace, the rollers of his bit champing over and over in the animal's blissful content.

They reached the flat of the valley and rode down the length of the ditch that served the grainfield in lieu of a fence. They came in time to a dozen long and rakish wagons, with canvas covers over their bows, drawn up in a loose circle. Within the circle were fires and a great scattering of gear of all sorts and a number of people. Beyond, on the slope of a hill, grazed a band of horses in charge of a mounted man. Leaning against the wagon wheels on the outside of the circle nearest the visitors, squatted on their heels in the shade of the wagon bodies, perched on the wagon tongues, were over a score of men. They wore broad slouch hats, floppy from use, dark garments. In their hands they one and all carried long-barreled rifles or other weapons. Their attitude was of stolid expectation.

Andy's eyes roved keenly over every detail of the scene before him. Leslie's intuitions, sharpened by the thrill of expectation, could almost feel the working of the strange, sure mechanism of the man's perceptions. He was suddenly seized by a great curiosity, for he sensed here a skill of which he knew nothing.

"What do you make of them, sir?" He could not restrain his inquiry.

"They—someone—knows their business," muttered Andy, as though more than half to himself. "They've fit Injuns—or some of them have. The way they got their wagons"—he yielded to Leslie's unspoken but evident question—"the way they got together to meet us—must have scouts out to watch what we're up to—rifles, none of your farmer blunderbusses." He turned to Leslie. "I don't *sabe* this," he confessed. He touched the *palomino* with his heel. "Let's go see what it is all about. Don't seem reasonable-like, but maybe we'll have to strike the post a'ter all."

"The post?" echoed Leslie.

"War post," said Andy briefly.

"You mean fight?"

Andy grinned wholeheartedly at the expression of his face.

"Not right this minute, bub," said he.

IX

THEY rode up to the lounging men and stopped. Leslie thought he had never seen such a hard-bitten lot. They were all over the average in height. They wore slouch hats and clothes of homespun, the trousers tucked into the tops of rough cowhide boots. In or on the belts at their waists was a variety of knives and pistols. Their lean cheeks were stubbled or completely unshaven. They said nothing, nor moved, but stared with a sullen hostility, their jaws moving slowly on their tobacco quids. Beyond them, inside the circle formed by the covered wagons, Leslie saw women and girls in shapeless calico and sunbonnets and small children in single garments; and all these, too, had stopped short in whatever they were doing and had frozen to immobility and now stared. It seemed to the young man that he could almost feel the physical impact of those challenging eyes.

"You men are welcome to camp on my property as long as it suits you," said Andy clearly. "Keep your animals out of the wheat. Clean up after you when you move on."

His words fell without effect, as though into the darkness of a bottomless well. No one moved; it almost seemed that no one winked. Except for the slow movement of their jaws these might have been figures of wax. Finally one spat, passed his hand over his beard.

"We ain't aimin' to move on," said this one with a certain leaden finality. "This ain't yore land."

"No?" said Andy softly.

"No," returned the man.

Several of the loungers stirred slightly, as though in expectation. Andy made no reply. He waited.

"You greasers are licked," said the man after a time. "You don't own this kentry no more. This bottom land is ours. Keep off'n it. We don't like tres-passers."

"Are you the boss of this outfit?" Andy's voice was mild, devoid of resentment.

"Ef'n I'm not, you kin talk to me till the boss comes along."

"Well, I want you to understand that you are on private land, that you are trespassing, and I serve you warning to get out."

One of the younger men laughed briefly but instantly sobered. The spokesman spat insolently in the direction of the *palomino*. Lucero tossed his head with a snort. Andy soothed the animal with the palm of his hand.

"Look yere, greaser," said the Missourian, "we don't want no trouble, but we ain't dodging any. We're American citizens, and we know our rights. This yere ain't yore land. It belongs to the guv'ment, and we've tuk up on it accordin' to law, and yere we're goin' to stay. We don't aim to move for your say-so, and we don't aim to bother you. Not while you behave. Is that clear?"

"Just one thing," said Andy. "Why do you say it's not my land?"

"Because it ain't!" cried one of the younger men fiercely. "Ain't we done conkered the kentry!"

But the leader silenced him with a gesture.

"Ransom!" He raised his voice. "Hi! Ransom! Whar be ye?"

From one of the covered wagons on the far side of the

circle Ransom slowly descended, rubbing his eyes ostentatiously, as though just awakened, though both Andy and Leslie knew he had not been asleep. He sauntered across the circle, slipped between the wagons, and surveyed the two visitors with an insolent but veiled triumph.

"This yere jay bird wants to know why this yere ain't his land," said the Missourian. "You tell him."

Ransom bared his fangs with an evil smile. He rattled off an impressive-sounding rigmarole of technicalities, to which his own audience listened with profound respect and as profound incomprehension; Leslie with growing indignation and an almost uncontrollable urge to break in with what even his slender legal knowledge told him was good refutation; Andy, apparently, not at all. Before Ransom had finished his speech the *ranchero* lifted his bridle hand. The *palomino* half reared, carried his forelegs about in a complete half circle until he faced the other way, set his hoofs down as lightly as a thistledown, paced away. Andy did not look back. Leslie followed, somewhat awkwardly, the spectacle of Ransom's significant leer in his eyes.

Ransom watched the pair of them ride away. He spat.

"What'd I tell you?" he challenged. "He won't make no trouble. And if he does———"

Stampede

"I reckon we-all can take keer of it," said the bearded man, not without a certain dignity.

2

Leslie was boiling over with indignation, which he voiced as soon as he caught up. This whole business was outrageous: it would not stand for any moment in any court in the land; even assuming the title was defective, it had not been declared so, and the land could, by no theory, be considered open to filing or to settlement until so declared; a good lawyer, a writ of trespass, or ejectment, or whatever it was ... So far from his sense of civilized equities, the orderliness of his education, the smattering of legalisms as to the land he had picked up from his week in Judge McCain's office. He fell silent. He saw that Andy was paying to him no more attention than to the wind through the trees.

They drew rein at the edge of the wide live oak before the door of the *casa*. With the exception of certain of the *vaqueros* out on the range, of the *mozas* at the stream bank, and of the Indians of the *milpas*, the entire personnel of the *rancho* had gathered, waiting for news of the *patrón's* excursion. They stood about, and near the doorway of the *casa* were Carmel and Djo and his sister and a few of the more privileged of the house servants. They were silent with anxiety, for none knew what this excursion might portend, though all had heard rumors, until now little considered, of similar doings nearer the Bay.

Andy paid them no attention. His eyes passed them over, identified Djo. He summoned Djo with a slight lift of the head and dismounted. A *mozo* led away the *palomino* and Leslie's horse. After a moment of hesitation Leslie followed his host.

Andy squatted on his heels, his forearms on his knees, his hands hanging. Djo took a similar position opposite him. Leslie, to whom this posture was impossible for long at a time, leaned against the tree trunk. As Andy talked he scraped together bits of twig, of bark, of dried leaves from the ground litter, heaped them in a little pile. He produced a pipe, which he lighted with a flint and steel and a string of tinder, and when he had finished this he ignited the heap of debris he had scraped together, so that in a moment it burst into flame, and blue smoke arose composedly in the air currents of the branches overhead. He did this as though mechanically, and thereafter from time to time he reached out his long arm at appropriate intervals to retrieve another bit of fuel by which to keep alive his council fire. For that was what it was. In the fire and the pipe, had Leslie known it, he was seeing welling up from the man's subconscious, in response to emergency, old forgotten ceremony that had met emergency in a past long gone.

Andy talked directly to Djo, who listened gravely and without comment.

"Twenty-two men," said he. "Fourteen grooved bar'ls and some smooth bores. Sixteen wagons. *Remuda* on the sidehills—less'n a hundred hosses. No oxen. Three men that's seen sarvice on the plains—rest greenhorns, exceptin' what experience they got crossing. Used to backwoods, though. Squirrel and deer shots." He spoke slowly, in a voice and vernacular whose smooth drawl Leslie did not recognize, for it, too, was reminiscent of old, less grammatical days. Djo nodded understanding of the points raised and the conclusions reached. Leslie did not understand some of them. He marveled at the man's detailed observation, the things Andy had noticed while he himself had been preoccupied with indignations. Shortly Andy had finished, methodically, his recital of what he had seen. As simply he went on to his deductions and conclusions, speaking always slowly, detachedly, almost as though of things that did not concern him, but which he must proffer.

"This man Ransom," he said, "he's back of them. He

brought 'em here. It's his way of making trouble, of getting even. That's why he brought 'em so far; brought 'em here. That's what he's been up to. That's why he came here before. That's why he was here a while back, before the rodeo, when you boys saw him." Andy's eyes were blank with inner concentration. "He's no farmer," he continued after a moment. "And he's no fighter," he added. He puffed thoughtfully on the almost extinct tobacco in his pipe until it was well alight again. "He wa'n't looking for a pot shot at you boys," he resumed, "though he might have took one ef'n he'd had a good chance. No, he was a'ter other game. Scouting around. The lay of the land. And I'd bet you this: I'd bet if you'd have rummaged his possible sack you'd have found he'd a copy of the records—like Leslie has of Constansio's. He knowed more about those fuzzy boundaries than you boys did—finding out whether he had a good excuse to come." Andy spoke slowly, as though groping a way.

Leslie started forward to interpose. He wanted to repeat that the mere indeterminateness of the grant, of the *diseño,* meant nothing until illegality was properly established. He stopped short as though checked by a curb. He looked about at the waiting people. They stood with scarce a motion, without a sound, their eyes fixed upon the squatting figures on either side the tiny fire. From the doorway the women of the household likewise watched, with the same attentive suspense. Leslie had a curious feeling that he had been saved from a grave indiscretion of some sort.

"And he's no farmer," the slow drawl resumed after a moment. "He did not come to farm, like these other critters. He came for pay. And he came here to git even. So," was Andy's unexpected conclusion, "it ain't him we got to bother about. Now we got that straight."

He tapped out the ashes from his pipe. The action seemed to terminate that something with which Leslie could not interfere. He spoke up at last. Andy turned on him blank eyes of total incomprehension.

"Lawyer?" he repeated. "Lawyer? Ef'n I can't take keer of what belongs to me, I certainly ain't going running to ary lawyer! This gang's got no right now to whar they are, title or no title, boundaries or no boundaries—ain't that what you said?"

"Yes, but——"

"Then, by the 'tarnal, off they get, and thar's no more to be said!" Andy for the first time spoke with a deadly unleashed passion. But immediately he regained his sardonic calm. "We'll talk lawyer when the time comes," said he.

3

Andy seemed to regain touch with his immediate surroundings. Up to this moment it was as though he had been communing with himself.

"Come," said he, "let's hold council."

He looked about him, searching identities among those who stood in expectation.

"Panchito," he summoned, "and you, Benito. And Means. Where is Abel Means?"

"Coming, boss," said the old ex-sailor and millwright, moving into view.

Without command a *mozo* stepped forward with an armful of fuel. He rebuilt carefully the haphazard little fire into an orderly blaze and withdrew. Andy and Djo arose from squatting on their heels and took their places on one of the wooden benches. Those summoned occupied the other, holding their broad hats in their laps. At a gesture of invitation from Djo, Leslie joined the *ranchero* and his son. The gathered peoples of the *rancho* held their places, gazing with a dumb expectancy. In the doorway Leslie caught a glimpse of the Doña Carmel, her smooth brows knit with repressed anxiety, and he thought it strange she was not included in this conference that must affect her so deeply. He could not know that again he witnessed a reversion to old days, to old habits so deeply grooved that in emergency life flowed through them as naturally as waters in a channel. If Leslie had possessed that sort of second sight, so that realities had clothed themselves to him in their outward seeming, his vision would have been of cowled warriors, and the smoke of the calumet rising to mingle with the smoke of the ceremonial fires, and in the background the women who could take no part in council.

Matters, said Andy, speaking in Spanish, are thus and so. He described the situation as he had observed it in the squatters' camp.

"There are of them," he enumerated, "twenty-two men armed to fight. We have here three—four," he corrected himself, "who know the business of the rifle and pistol, and a dozen with lance and *reata*. To use the lance and *reata* one must ride close, and these men are skilled *rifleros*. We cannot attack them. Nor," said Andy, "if they should themselves attack the *rancho* could we prevent its capture. It is possible we might hold them from the *casa* for a time, but only for a time." He glanced from one to the other, assuring himself that he was fully understood. "It is not probable that they will attack us unless we provoke them to it. Therefore, that is the first thing that must be told the people: that they must do nothing to provoke these men. That is understood?"

He challenged each with a look. They nodded.

"Each is responsible for his own people," said Andy. "Until the time comes when we are ready, all must go on as usual. Is there anyone on the *rancho* who cannot be trusted to be quiet? One word of what we shall be doing," he warned, "one word to make these people suspicious that we are not afraid of them, that we have not given up because we are afraid of them, that they aren't going to have their own way—they'll be up here. You, Panchito, your *vaqueros*. Are they all to be trusted?"

"As myself, *patrón*," growled the major-domo.

"How about your people, Abel?"

The millwright spat copiously into the fire.

"I'll answer for what men there be," said he in English, "but I won't be responsible for no women."

"This isn't women's business," said Andy. "Benito?"

The moonfaced master of the fields and dairies smiled comfortably, waved his hands. He seemed to think this sufficient reply. When Andy spoke next it was with the staccato snap of command.

Stampede

"Three of the *vaqueros* will come to me after dark. Mount them well. They will carry messages," he said to Panchito. "Eight of your best Indians"—he turned to Benito—"they will watch these people, two by two, for four hours at a time for each two. One will come to me if there is anything unusual, while the other remains to watch. They must not be discovered. Abel," he said to Means, still in Spanish, so the others might understand, "your business is around and near the *casa*. You're *sabio*. Leave all your other affairs for this: that you watch always that matters go on as they have always done and that nothing happens out of the ordinary. Three of these men are old Indian fighters," he added in English; "I can see that, and it mout be they'd do a little scouting on their own hook. Leastwise for a day or two till they're satisfied we're skeered to make trouble. And you tell 'em, specially the youngsters, that if I hear of ary one of 'em as much as *lookin'* down that hill, I'll skin 'em alive."

"You won't need to," said Means grimly; "they'll be already skun."

"That is all for now, until we are ready," said Andy, again in Spanish. "It is important that we have time. If these *ladrónes* should get it into their heads to attack us before we are ready, we would have to get out. And the saints know what they might not do here." He looked about at the *casa* and its surroundings. "Has anyone anything to say?"

The *californios* looked questioningly at one another.

"Are we then not to fight, señor?" growled Panchito.

It was Abel Means who spoke up before Andy could reply.

"You'll get plenty of fighting; don't worry," said he dryly.

" 'He who would enter a low door must stoop,' " quoted Benito comfortably.

Andy looked at him with approval.

"That's it," said he, "and this one may be so low you may have to crawl on your belly. Very well, crawl."

"Señor Padre"—it was Djo, speaking up rather hesitatingly and using the ceremonial form.

"Yes?"

"My mother, my sister. Would it not be well that we send them for a while to visit at the *hacienda* or at Los Madrones with my uncle Ramon and the Doña Conchita?"

"No," said Andy.

"But if these *ladrónes* do attack us—and they here ——"

"No," repeated Andy. His eyes, it seemed to Leslie, were like flints, so hard were their outer surfaces. But after a moment he yielded to explanation. "If it warn't for that old he-coon and his pair of Injun fighters, I'd say yes. But they'll be watchin' for a move like that. We've got to keep 'em quiet, and nothing will do that better than keeping our women and children here." He laid his hand on Djo's arm. "I know, son. It's dangerous. But this is war. We've struck the post. And don't you worry"—he extended his great fist, opened and shut it slowly—"I aim to take keer of my own."

X

LESLIE seemed to himself to be living in a strange, unreal world of double consciousness. On the surface things went on much as usual on the *rancho*. It stirred to life about daylight; it moved with spacious leisure through the day; it withdrew early to the darkness of repose. The sun soaked the hours that passed to the droning of bees. The people rode or walked about their affairs gently, with space for the leisure of little courtesies. Down by the wash stones at the stream bed the *mozas* laughed and chattered. The *vaqueros* rode out, or in, to a jangling of spurs and bit chains. In the bottom lands Benito's Indians bent over their hoes. Benito himself went about his leisurely preparations to harvest the barley. About the *casa* the numerous retainers attended their business, chattering soft-voiced, or singing. The Doña Carmel's gracious figure was everywhere about the place, her smooth brow placid beneath her smoothed hair. The girl, Amata, was much with her.

This was one of the small differences—that for the time being the girl, Amata, rode no more abroad. Nor did the *ranchero* himself. Andy sat most of the day on one of the benches beneath the live-oak tree, where he smoked and talked occasionally to people who came to him. But such trifles could be noticeable only to a familiar. To a stranger it must have seemed that affairs moved in the quiet old routine.

But Leslie sensed beneath this surface of accustomedness a vibrant taut swiftness of action, an inner expectation behind the drowsy eyes, gathered muscles beneath the slow, lazy movement of life. Something peeped out from studied reticences. For nobody talked. They waited.

2

The surface was only a surface. Surprising things sometimes thrust themselves above it for a moment. As when Leslie, restless for some reason, and unable to sleep, arose from his bed and wandered outside the *casa* in the thought that the night air might make him drowsy, and so came face to face with Djo. Or rather Djo came face to face with him as he stood motionless in the shadow. Leslie was startled. After a moment's hesitation Djo burst out laughing. He choked back the sound.

"What on earth!" cried Leslie, dumfounded.

"Hush!" warned Djo. He seized Leslie by the elbow and drew him down the colonnade and into his own room. He shut the heavy door carefully. Then he laughed again at Leslie's expression.

Djo was dressed in black, from head to foot. On his feet he wore deerskin moccasins. His face and hands had been rubbed with charcoal, and from this mask his gray eyes and white teeth flashed grotesquely.

"What on earth!" repeated Leslie helplessly.

Djo explained with relish, while he splashed water from the ewer into the basin. Scouting . . . the squatters' camp . . . crawling, inch by inch, until he lay fairly inside the enemy lines, so near he could hear the men's breathing. The most exciting fun in the world! Djo spoke with pride of the *ranchero's* confidence in him to do this delicate job.

"My father trained me to do it," said he. "My father

learned these things from the Indians, over the mountains. No *californio* could do it. I have once—when I was a boy —made my way into the *milpas* by daylight, and the Indians and Benito working there, and carried away vegetables. When I played *wild man*. I'll tell it to you someday. That was just a game. If I was caught at it, it would not matter much: I just lost the game. But now"—Djo chuckled—"I wonder what *would* happen?"

"Does the Doña Carmel know of this?"

"Heaven forbid!" Djo was alarmed. "You must not breathe a word to her."

"I won't," promised Leslie.

Djo had finished scrubbing his face. He sat on the edge of his bed.

"It's not difficult now," said he. "There's no sentry. They've made up their minds we've knuckled down. They stood sentries at first. And they're sound sleepers. I'm more scared of the dogs. Though they don't pay much attention to the dogs, either. They're always answering back at the coyotes."

"How long you been at this?" asked Leslie, astonished.

"Every night."

"But why?" To Leslie it seemed that one, or at most two, visits should be ample to gather any desired information. What could there be to know? "What are you looking for? What do you do?"

"I know," said Djo impressively, "exactly where every man sleeps, and how he sleeps, and how easy he is to wake. It wasn't two days before I knew exactly the habits of the place. I could go in there blindfolded and lay my hand on any man—or woman or child, for that matter—you have a mind to name. I know just where each man keeps his weapons, and how. I know where each horse is tied. By golly, I mighty near know where every man lays his quid when he turns in!" He laughed to conceal his genuine pride of achievement; for, though he was pleased to impress his friend, he did not wish to appear to do so.

"What you keep on going for, if you knew all about it in two days?" asked Leslie sensibly. "You're bound to get caught."

"I won't get caught," said Djo, who was a trifle above himself from the release of strain.

"Well, a dog'll bite you, anyway," insisted Leslie.

Djo laughed. "That might be," he admitted. "I'll tell you. My father sends me back to see if there is any change. What I mean is, if the arrangements are always the same, or if they shift around any—if a man sleeps here one night and there the next—that sort of thing."

"I see," said Leslie. "Do they?"

"Not to amount to anything."

"How long do you keep this up?"

"I don't know. Until my father tells me. I don't know. He does not talk."

"I wish I knew enough to help," said Leslie from a mixture of humility and envy. He hesitated before possible indiscretion. "What's he going to do? Do you know?"

"Nobody knows but *mi padre*," Djo answered readily enough. "He is like that." He yawned. "Golly, I'm sleepy!" said he.

3

Every few hours, with the change of watch, the two Indians who had lain in the brush spying reported to Andy, sitting under the live-oak tree. At irregular intervals one of those on duty came in to tell of the departure of some of the intruders from their camp. Then Andy sent out one of his people to discover at least the direction of their errand. This was done not by following after them, which must surely be discovered, for the *californios* were little skilled in concealment, but by arranging to cut across their trail, or to meet them as though by accident.

The excursions proved invariably to be in search of meat. The hills were full of deer. Most of the older bucks had by now climbed to the higher peaks, but the lower country still harbored many spikes and forked horns; and there were, of course, plenty of does. The latter were heavy with fawn, but the Missourians made no distinctions. Curiously, this appeared to arouse Djo's indignation—at least his surface indignation—more even than the trespass. Djo had been brought up by Andy in the utilitarian sportsmanship of the pioneer and Indian, and it was so deeply ingrained as to have ceased to be conscious. He reacted as automatically as to an instinct. Andy stopped sending him on these errands. Djo alone of the ranch people was able actually to follow unobserved and be witness of whatever was doing, but this was unimportant. Few days passed without such an expedition toward the hills. The parties were generally of a half dozen or so—probably for protection against possible "treachery" by the ranch people—with pack horses. The faint far sound of their rifles could be heard at intervals throughout the day. They brought back the pack horses laden, and often some of the horsemen carried a carcass before him across his saddle. These small coast-range blacktails did not dress a hundred pounds. First and last they slaughtered a great many deer, and day by day the sound of the rifles sounded fainter as the game was decimated or withdrew from the nearer hills.

Djo chafed bitterly, for to him its game was a part of Folded Hills. But Andy, remembering perhaps old days of "living on the country," showed no impatience. Indeed he seemed impervious to indignations that periodically shook those around him. He appeared to survey them from a preoccupation in more important things. Panchito's men found indubitable evidence that the meat parties were, at least occasionally, killing cattle. Andy nodded.

"I've been expecting that," he said to Djo and Leslie; "the deer are getting scarce—or being druv back. They got to eat, and cattle are easier."

"What shall we do, señor?" asked Panchito.

"Nothing," said Andy. "Nothing!" he repeated in the sharp accents of command as he saw Panchito's face. The *vaquero* rode away grumbling.

Down in the bottom lands, the Indians reported, the intruders were cutting down the trees. They were building houses, corrals, splitting rails for fences! A madness, señor, what with the adobe underfoot and greasewood at hand, and a ditch needs only digging! Nevertheless, if one listened, one could hear the rhythmical ringing clop of the axes. This stirred Carmel as the sounds of the distant rifles among the deer stirred Djo. These lower groves were dear to her, for there the subsoil drainage from the hills nourished the oaks and sycamores and cottonwoods to a greater height and size, and it was there were held the *meriendas*. The sound of the axes—like the sound of the rifles—was so very faint and far that the slightest nearer noises, a preoccupation of mind even, were sufficient to submerge it. One had to listen to hear it at all. Yet it seemed to Carmel that she must listen and that each blow was struck at her heart.

"Cannot we do something to stop it?" she cried.

"Not yet," said Andy.

And the placid and comfortable Benito came wringing his hands. The horses of these *ladrónes* had invaded the lower wheat and barley fields. They had broken down the ditches. They were trampling the nearly ripened grain, bedding in it, eating it down like grass.

"And the hills fat with *alfileria, señor!*" lamented Benito.

Should he not send down *los indios* to drive the animals out?

"Not yet," said Andy. And Benito, too, went away sullen, for he had come to Folded Hills when they were wilderness, and the grainfields had become more his children than the dozen or so grown men and women who carried his name.

So the anger of each grew, nourished by his own, which was perhaps what Andy intended; or his reticence until the time of accomplishment might have been a throwback to old days when a warrior kept his counsel, or it might, more simply, have been a precaution against some tattle reaching the squatters untimely. Though everyone on the *rancho* knew that the *patrón* was not one to sit tamely under aggression.

Only to Abel Means, the millwright, did Andy partly open his mind. The ex-sailor showed no curiosity. Andy knew he never talked, even of unimportant things. Yet not even to Abel Means did the *ranchero* disclose his full thought until the thought was formed. Then he summoned the millwright, and the two sat under the oak, their heads together. Occasionally Means nodded or spat in the fire. Now that the time for action was nearing Andy spread his plan out, not so much for the opinion of criticism as for his own examination.

"You know and I know, Abel," said Andy, exaggerating his trapper drawl after his fashion when talking to old-timers, like Means, "that twenty good men with rifles, ahind wagons, can stand off a power of people like ours. The *californio* is a brave man and a good fighter, no matter what they say. He's not skeered to die ef'n he means business. But he's got no arms, and he hasn't got the habit of using arms. Greatest hoss fighters in the world, as I've always said, give 'em a chance. I suppose we could get together enough men, even without rifles, to ride over 'em. But we'd get a lot of men killed doing it. No question of that. These Missouri backwoodsmen are good shots. So I've been studying on something else."

"Yes?" said Abel Means.

"Ef'n we had a half-dozen more used to the rifle and trained up to Injun fighting, we could make it. I sent Djo down to look 'em over. I figgered maybe we could do a night surprise, or early morning. But Djo and I are about the only ones around here could make it to get close enough without being diskivered. You couldn't do it?" he said on a note of inquiry.

"I'm a sailor," said Abel Means, who had not touched foot to deck for eighteen years.

"Even three'd be too few, anyway. Needs at least a half a dozen to hold 'em till the riders could get in. Then I tried to figger a way to git 'em out of that on hossback. Ef'n we could git 'em on hossback out in the open, I'd guarantee to deliver 'em, tied up, in ten minutes. Ef'n it was only these backwoodsmen, that would be easy: they're terrible greenhorns when it comes to open-kentry fighting. But they got three pretty *sabe* plainsmen in the lot. They wouldn't toll out of cover for a cent, not if they knew their business like I think they do. So I let that go. And then it struck me that a man does his best when he works with nature, uses the strong p'ints for him instead of agin him. These folks have two strong p'ints—their rifles and their three plainsmen. So I'm going to use 'em."

"Anon?" queried Means, justifiably puzzled.

"A plainsman don't know a thing about cattle, but he knows a heap about buffalo," said Andy. He bent closer, speaking low, glancing about from time to time to be sure nobody could hear.

"Have you got enough?" asked Means.

"Enough are on the way," said Andy.

XI

THE day after this conference a *vaquero* rode in at full speed to report a great cloud of dust on the slopes of the ranges toward Jolon, as though an army were advancing.

"Or maybe cattle, fool," said Panchito scornfully. "Go back to your business."

By noon the dust cloud had rolled lazily forward until its fog was on the lower hills of the *rancho*. At this time Ramon Rivera rode in at an easy lope, a *vaquero* at his heels. He swung from his saddle a little heavily, for Ramon had not Andy's youthful hard condition, but with a bubbling effervescence of spirit that was still young.

Stampede

"We come, *amigo!*" he cried gaily. "All I could gather so quickly. And fifteen good riders. Where would you have them?"

"The upper *prado;* Panchito will show your men."

"Shall they be held?"

"Let them graze. But keep some riders with them to see that they do not scatter too much. It may be two days yet."

Ramon nodded, turned to give instructions to his *vaquero,* who rode away.

"And the others?" Andy asked, when the man had departed.

"They come, and gladly," said Ramon in English. "Tomorrow, I think. Don José Constansio, yes; the Cermenos, yes; also those from El Chapitel *rancho,* and those others those could tell. Those three will bring the many cow, as you have said, but I think also will come a many of men from the *ranchos* that are too far to send the cow."

Andy looked anxious, Ramon noticed.

"Do not be escare, *valedor*," said he reassuringly. "Nobody know the why but you, but me, but the Don José, but Don Nicolas Cermenos"—he counted each on a finger—"and Don Pedro of El Chapitel. Just those. All other come because it is told that Don Largo have *matanza*"

—Ramon laid his finger aside his nose—"*matanza*—what you call? The killing—of many cow. Oh yes! That Don Largo give the *fiesta,* ask them to come to the killing."

"*Fiesta?*" Andy was still more uneasy. "This is no time for women."

"No woman; man *fiesta*," Ramon said solemnly, then laughed. "It is all right, *amigo*. Nobody going talk."

"I hope not," grumbled Andy. "Well, come on; Carmel will want to see you."

"You tell Carmelita?" asked Ramon.

"No, nobody. Not even Djo."

Ramon shook his head.

"You are like—what you call—the clam, *valedor,* and that is not good for all peoples, only for those you do not love. You mus' tell Carmelita," he said earnestly. "It is very bad if you do not tell to Carmelita."

"I don't want to worry her too soon," muttered Andy.

"He don' want to worry her too soon," mocked Ramon. "You titch me many thing, *valedor,* but I think I'm always going to titch you about the womans. You go tell Carmel, *pronto,* right off queek!"

2

So it happened that Carmel was present at the strange council or gathering in the *sala* of Folded Hills the following evening. All the candles of sperm wax in the sconces along the wall were lighted as for a *fiesta*. The long room was full. Andy stood in front of the empty fireplace beneath the long Boone rifle that hung, almost symbolically, across the pegs over his head. In chairs sat various grandees of the neighborhood—and some from a considerable distance. There were of course Ramon Rivera of Los Madrones and Don José Constansio of Alisal from the Jolon Plateau and, standing back of them, Basil Rivera and Samuel Constansio, their sons; the Cermenos —father and three sons—the six from the *rancho* of El Chapitel, Calderon and his tall boys from Soledad. But also, in the big armchair, ordinarily Andy's evening comfort, rested the still-straight and erect figure of Don Sylvestro, who had ridden from the *hacienda,* apparently without fatigue in spite of his age. He sat quietly, stroking his long white beard, his young eyes, in which harbored a relish of expectation, traveling from one to the other. With him had ridden the elder of Carmel's brothers,

Ygnacio, and the youngest, Felipe. Cristobal dwelt now near San Luis Obispo.

"I could bring no cattle, *hijo mío*," Don Sylvestro had said to Andy. "It is too far. But I have brought some *vaqueros*. Use them as you will."

"This is, then, a matter of common news," said Andy, half vexed.

"But no!" Ramon hastened to assure him. "It was I. I sent by an especial messenger. You would not have my papa miss such essport?" he asked reproachfully.

"No one else?" probed Andy with suspicion.

"No-no-no!" cried Ramon. "Only those you have told me!"

But in the *sala,* beside these of the *hidalgo* class, were a dozen or more grave-faced, hard-bitten riders of the range, the chief *vaqueros,* the trusted men of the *hacendados.* They leaned against the wall, without expression, without comment, their hands crossed before them beneath their wide hats, waiting in respectful silence.

The windows of the *sala* were open for coolness and air, for the night was warm and the gathering overcrowded for the room. A guard, or sentry, one of Panchito's choosing, paced slowly back and forth outside lest any of the numerous people should approach within earshot, for this council was secret. From the direction of the hills came the bellowing and lowing of cattle, in all keys and tones, so that the composite sound was like the sweep and roll of a mighty organ, and almost one could feel a faint trembling of the solid earth.

Andy spoke. He addressed them all but deferred especially to Don Sylvestro and Don José, who sat side by side. With the opening brief phrases, which pointed out the need of doing something, they nodded agreement.

"We know of Don Luis Peralta," said Don Sylvestro simply.

"We have come to your summons, Don Andreo," Constansio pointed out.

They listened attentively while Andy sketched, as he had to Abel Means, the formidable character of the Missourians and the certainty of heavy loss in a direct attack. Some of the younger men growled at this.

"If you lead us, Don Largo, we shall ride them down!" cried one. The rest murmured eager assent.

Andy flashed a look in their direction.

"We have no arms," said he. "That would be suicide for many. But here is what we shall do," said he. "Listen to that." He paused, and the deep diapason of the cattle rolled through the momentary silence. "There are twenty thousand cattle there in the hills. We shall drive them down the valley. We shall *drive* them down the valley," he added significantly.

Like most naturally adventurous men, Andy had a hidden but powerful sense of the dramatic. He stopped with the simple statement, allowing it time to kindle in these men's comprehension. A breathless pause ensued. The young men turned to each other, their eyes alight.

"The cattle are our weapon!" cried Ygnacio Rivera.

"Exactly," said Andy.

He waited for the hubbub to die, glancing with an easy humor from the excited and wholly enthusiastic younger men to the grave countenances of the elder. But it was to neither he finally appealed.

"Panchito," he summoned.

"Señor!" The head *vaquero,* surprised, but with full composure, straightened his tall form.

"What think you?" asked Andy.

Panchito looked about the company in deprecation of the prominence into which he had been thrust over his betters. Nevertheless he answered directly enough.

"It is the señor's idea to drive these cattle down the valley and over these *ladrónes?*" he asked, or rather stated. "This cannot be done, señor."

"Why not?" asked Andy.

"It would be impossible to drive cattle over the wagons, señor, no matter how rapidly they are pressed. They will turn away, or they will split in two parts and pass around, and there is no power that could push them over wagons. At night, if they are very frightened, perhaps a few, señor, but only a few." He spoke regretfully, respectfully, but with the firm assurance of the expert; and his companion *vaqueros* along the wall nodded their heads in confirmation. "Yes, that is so, señor." And the *hacendados* nodded too, and the young men eyed Panchito, resentful that he must destroy so gorgeous a conception, but with a reluctant assent. One turned to Panchito direct.

"When they are away from their wagons," said he. "They do not live always in their accursed wagons, *madre de Dios!*"

Andy shook his head, answering for Panchito.

"That would be so, were it not for one thing," said he. "There are with these people those who have lived in the Indian country and have learned the wisdom of battle. It has been brought to them that we hold a great *matanza*, and I think they believe that. If it were not for these three of whom I speak, we might, as Don Gasper says, ride them down with the cattle when they were away from their encampment. But as long as there are so many of us *californios* gathered near, no matter for what reason, they will not stir from their shelter. These wise ones will see to that. Is that what you are thinking, Panchito?"

"*Sí, señor.*"

"Well, you are right." Andy turned to Leslie. "Do you understand what we're saying?" he asked, still in Spanish.

"Pretty well," said Leslie in English.

"Speak Spanish," said Andy. "Did you get what Panchito said about not being able to drive cattle across the wagons?"

"Yes, I understood that."

"Did you know that before?"

"No," said Leslie. "I do not know much about cattle," he confessed.

"Nor do these others." Andy turned to the room at large. "But"—he held them for a moment before proceeding—"they all know buffalo. And buffalo, when they get started, will run over anything. Unless they are split or turned. This can be done. It is done by shooting down the leaders. Here is my plan."

He looked about him at the attentive faces, collected himself.

"It is a chance," he warned, "but it may succeed. In any

case it will help. It will be better than a direct attack against riflemen behind wagons.

"We have together, in the hills beyond the *matanza* grounds, somewhere near twenty thousand cattle. Tomorrow we shall cut out about two thousand and drive them against the wagons. We shall stampede them, rush them. To these robbers it will seem that they are to be trampled down. They know buffalo; they do not know cattle. They will shoot, as they would shoot into a buffalo stampede. The cattle will turn or will divide to left and right. They will go by."

"Hah!" surmised Don Sylvestro. "The rifles will all be emptied. We shall ride in."

"They might all be emptied," admitted Andy, "but I think not. And for this reason: these plains fighters, these three, have been brought up on stratagems of that sort. The Indians use the stampede—of buffalo and of horses. Some of the rifles will not be fired. They will be kept in reserve for such an attack and until the others can be reloaded."

"What then?" asked the *hidalgo*.

"Another two thousand, and another, and another, as rapidly as one can follow the other."

The younger men were looking toward each other ecstatically. Ramon, the ever youthful, gave them voice.

"*Holá!*" he cried. "But that will be sport!"

But the older heads saw farther.

"To what end, Don Andreo? How will the twentieth occasion differ from the first?" Asked Don José Constansio courteously, "Is it your thought that thus these will exhaust their powder?"

Andy shook his head.

"No, señor," he disclaimed, "for twenty rounds could not have that effect."

"The cattle could be gathered and driven again," said Ramon.

"With due respect, señor, one such run will cure them of running for that day," suggested Calderon.

"Then the next day," insisted Ramon stubbornly. "These people do not fly like birds. They will be there."

"It would be impossible to hold so many cattle; the grass would be gone, and the water." Calderon was becoming just as obstinate.

"I think, señores, that Don Ramon's idea may be possible. But it is my hope that we shall not need it," Andy interposed to end the discussion. "I have not said all my plan."

"We will listen to Don Andreo," said Señor Rivera with authority.

"This maneuver I have told you," went on Andy. He spoke very slowly and distinctly, not only to reach the intelligences of the *vaqueros* against the wall, but also, Leslie felt gratefully, that he might follow the Spanish. "This maneuver might have several results. It is just possible that from pressure behind, or even from panic, that some of the cattle might dash against one or more of the wagons and overturn them. If that happens we must be ready to ride, to charge fast and get inside before the gap is closed. Once inside———"

"Viva!" cried Ramon, who already saw this as an accomplished fact. He subsided, like a small boy, under Don Sylvestro's glance.

"I do not think this will happen," continued Andy, "but we must be ready.

"It is also possible," he commented, "that after two, or three, or six, or eight times these *sabios* may conclude that we know nothing of stratagem, that we are simple *rancheros*, and that all we are doing is to try to trample them down. In that case, if the danger seems to them great enough, it might be that they *would* empty all their rifles and pistols. Also if that happens, we must be ready to charge before they can reload. We shall test that when the moment seems to me ripe." He paused, reflecting.

"And how will you do that test, Don Andreo?" the *hidalgo* asked.

"By sending in more cattle at one time. Or perhaps two lots quickly, one after the other, or even three. That I must decide when the time comes.

"But these things are only possibilities, which we will seize if they happen. But here, señores, is something sure. And it is on this I really count. Here is my plan.

"Before very long it must be that the attention of everybody will be fixed on the direction from which these cattle are coming. At first, perhaps, there will be men watching the other sides. But not for long, and not while the cattle are actually rushing upon them. That is human nature. Now it is my thought that each time, while attention is so fixed in one direction, that certain selected ones, on foot, draw nearer on all other sides. They must do so unseen. If any man is seen, then this part of the plan is lost. But it can be done. When these have come very close, then we shall stampede down the valley as many cattle as remain, and under cover of that these selected men shall thrust aside the wagons to make an entry for the horsemen."

"*Viva!*" cried Ramon again. "*Viva! Viva!*" echoed others. The idea seemed to nobody either fantastic or impracticable. Except perhaps the hardheaded old sailor, Abel Means. He looked across the room at Andy, shifted his quid speculatively, wondered just how mad the *patrón* might be.

"Crazy like an owl," concluded Abel Means finally, after due deliberation. "Couldn't git a sober white man to take such a fool notion serious enough to make it work. But with these yere lunatics most likely it will!" He looked at Andy with admiration. He turned to Leslie, who stood at his elbow. "It's going to be quite a circus, anyways," said he; "it's a great thing to know jist how to git the best out of what you got!"

"Eh?" Leslie was puzzled.

"Nothin'," said Abel Means.

3

The council did not break up until well after midnight. Once the main idea had been grasped, there were many details. There must be men to cut out, or collect, the requisite number for each drive or attack or demonstration. This would be dull work, hard work, but, worst of all, remote from the scene of the real excitement. Andy assigned this task to some of his own men, under Panchito, but he instantly took out some of the sting of disappointment by arranging for reliefs from among those who had already made a drive. There must be men, a number of groups of men, to fill this latter function: a half dozen to each band Andy considered sufficient to keep them going once the cattle had been started down the valley by the combined crews awaiting their turn. Here would be the dash of riding and the honor and the glory of excitement, and every man present was eager to be assigned the captaincy of one of these groups. Andy picked swiftly and surely from the younger men, apparently at hazard, but actually with sense of their positions and abilities.

"You will pick your own men from among your own *vaqueros*," he told them. "What you are to do is to drive your cattle as straight and as fast as you can directly at the wagons. When they split or turn you are to get into the hills and out of range as quickly and as safely as you can. I am not going to tell you how. You will make your own arrangements and give your own orders. I trust to your skill and good sense not to lose any of your men."

He looked appraisingly from face to face.

"There must be a *capataz*," he said, "someone who must order when each band is to start. This man must be obeyed. I need one who will not lose his head from excitement and whose judgment is good. You, Panchito, shall be this *capataz*. I will talk with you later. You will instruct each of these *caballeros* when they shall start. And"—he turned to the *caballeros*—"what Panchito says, that shall you do, without question, for he shall be as myself." He held them, rather sternly, with his eye until he had caught their murmur of assent.

Abel Means was rubbing his hands slowly one over the other. He nudged Leslie in the ribs.

"Purty slick," he murmured to that young man. "Takes him to put a *vaquero* to bossing these young squirts and makin' 'em both like it. Panchito was feeling pretty sore being left in the rear. Now look at 'im!"

Leslie followed his indication. Certainly the carved wooden immobility of the *vaquero's* face had, for the first time in Leslie's experience, an expression.

The young men had been whispering together apart.

"Who shall be the first, señor?" one of them asked.

Andy ran his eyes over the faces turned toward him. Some were eager; some were belligerent; some were sullen. He checked, considering; for here, he sensed at once, were the makings of a petty jealousy.

"Why, señores," he said slowly, "it seems to me that that matter is beyond the decision of any of us. It is a question we must leave to chance, for one man could not reasonably be chosen before another. The name of each shall be written on a paper and shall be taken, one by one, from a *sombrero,* and the names shall be read out by the Doña Amata. Thus, señores, it shall be decided, for no true *caballero* will deny the words of a *doncellita.*" He looked toward the corner where sat Carmel and the little girl, smiling to himself at the stiffly erect pride of the latter at being thus singled out for a part in these proceedings. Carmel seized the opportunity to throw him a pleading glance. Djo's name had not yet been mentioned.

"I," said Andy, "shall be on the little hill on the other side of the valley, and just below the wagons. There I can watch. With me shall be all the *caballeros* and all of the other men not otherwise assigned. There shall gather those who have driven the cattle. The slope is wide and easy. Down it we shall ride, if a good chance offers, or if this plan works out."

"Señor," suggested young Basil Constansio, "if we were to wait until such time as these ones graze their horses, we could undoubtedly, by a sudden dash, stampede them."

"Undoubtedly, señor," agreed Andy courteously. "For that reason we shall make our first drive as early as possible so that the horses may remain in their possession. In that case it may be just possible that these people might be tempted to mount and ride out against us."

A murmur of appreciation arose, for no *californio* but considered, and justly so, that in open warfare on horseback, with his own weapons of lance and *reata,* he was more than a match, man for man, for any other race.

"You think of everything, Don Largo!" murmured Don Sylvestro.

"You understandin' this?" asked Means, aside.

"Most of it," replied Leslie.

"Wal," said Means disparagingly, "it takes a hossman to know good handling when he sees it."

"What do you mean?" Leslie was puzzled.

"Mebbe you've noticed that the *californios* are different," said Means and relapsed into grumpy silence.

There were further details—signals, warnings, questions to be answered. Amata must draw the lots. The party dispersed. But not to sleep. The young men designated sought out their men, made their selections among their *vaqueros,* gave instructions. Panchito aroused his *vaqueros*. The combined forces began, by the dim light of the stars, to gather together and separate into bands the bawling herds.

As soon as the last visitor had gone and Andy and Carmel were alone together, her placidity broke. She seized his arm in both her hands.

"And those who must crawl in the grass and lie hidden and make the hole in the wagon circle for the horsemen," she said tensely. "You did not name them!"

Andy grinned.

"You noticed that! Nobody else did. Glad they didn't. I didn't want to hurt anybody's feelings."

"Who is to do that?" She gave his arm a little shake. Her eyes were wide.

"There's only one who could," said Andy.

"Djo!"

Andy nodded. "Who else? He's well trained; he can do it," he said with simple pride.

"He will be killed," wailed Carmel, her head dropping. She threw his arm from her in a sudden passion. "You send him there—your own son—to be killed!"

"I'd do it myself," said Andy soberly, "but somebody's got to overlook the game, and there's nobody but me can do that. Same," he added, "as there's nobody but Djo to do this other job."

"He'll be killed! He'll be killed!"

Andy took her two wrists in his great hands.

"Look at me!" he commanded. "There! I don't think

Djo will be killed. I'm going to fix it to be as safe as I can. But this is war. And it's our war. A man must take his chance. If he don't he's not a man. And Djo's a man. I raised him to be a man." Andy stood tall and straight. His eyes grew vacant; his grasp on Carmel's wrists relaxed. He was looking across the years to a past so remote that his own eyes had never seen it. Yet it was for the moment as vivid to him as though the scene were enacting in the present. He seemed to himself, for that flash, to stand in the gloom and murk of a dark room so low that his head almost touched its beams, and narrow slits of light where its wall was pierced, and the sharp acrid tang of powder smoke, and the dim forms of men peering through the slits cuddling rifle stock to cheek, and the sharp crack of bullet and the dull thud of arrow searching the walls. All this was dim and as though inside himself, but one thing was clear and sharp, so that it seemed outside himself. And it came to him that this dauntlessness at his elbow had been his grandmother, the friend of Boone in the Dark and Bloody Ground; or perhaps, more widely, the women of the Burnetts who had fronted battle with their men. The moment passed. Andy sighed, drew Carmel gently to him.

"Djo will be all right," he said. "Our Lady will keep him safe, and the blessed saints."

XII

No ONE SLEPT. Those who had charge of the cattle had their work cut out for them. The others were too interested. Andy summoned to him one after the other of those responsible and went over with each separately, again and again, the few contingencies and the signals to be employed in the one event or the other: for a frontal attack in case a breech should be made in the defense of wagons, or if, in Andy's judgment, the firearms had all been discharged at the same time; for a rear attack when and if Djo's contingent had succeeded in doing their part, or if it seemed to Andy that for any other reason the moment was favorable. Each one's task in these simple maneuvers he assigned and caused each to repeat back his understanding. Andy knew well enough the impossibility of keeping such an undisciplined and excitable people closely to any rigid plan of action, but he had strong faith that if they were started out right, something favorable was sure to develop. As Means had hinted to Leslie, Andy had acquired an uncanny knowledge of his adopted people and how best to make use of them. It is doubtful if the hardheaded Indian fighters of his earlier life could have pumped up enough enthusiasm for so fantastic a scheme to have carried it through; nor, on the other hand, would the *californios* have had the tenacity and cold-blooded courage to stick out a day of siege warfare. But for something like this, with movement, and excitement, and an element of rivalry, and a considerable appeal to the imagination, the *californio* was the man. Leslie vibrated in sympathy to the lighthearted and eager impatience for the show to begin that animated into restless skylarking the young men, both *caballero* and *vaquero*, who were to take part in the drives.

He himself was to have no share in that. He was in a way disappointed, for he could imagine the wild, mad, blood-stirring rush and movement of such a unique charge. On the other hand, it would soon be over, and the participants must take their places in waiting. While Leslie, in company with Djo and Abel Means and two young Spanish lads, would be from start to finish in the thick of the action. Theirs was the responsible task of getting to the rear wagons unseen and, unseen, of drawing them aside for the charge of the horsemen.

Andy talked to them as a group together; all the others he had instructed only through their *capitáns*. Leslie was inclined to deprecate his own choosing.

"I'm no good at this scouting work," said he.

"You're one of the few around here who knows anything about shooting," said Andy, "and for the rest of it, you just follow close at Djo's heels, and you do the same thing he does, *and at exactly the same time.*" He emphasized strongly the latter point. He grinned. "Chance maybe to show what good is all that pistol palaver," said he. Andy was still tolerantly amused at the lad's shooting theories. He turned to Means. "Same to you, Abel. You're about the only other one on the *rancho* who can use firearms."

"I'm a sailor," grumbled Means; "I ain't no rifleman!"

"I know that," said Andy with another grin, "but you don't shut both eyes when you pull trigger."

The Spanish lads, one of whom was Benito's son, were

Stampede

to go along as man power to help move the wagons. They carried knives and *machetes*. They listened with shining eyes to their simple instructions. Andy slapped them on the back

"Show them what a *californio* is made of," said he.

"Now yere you are, Djo." Andy reverted to trapper talk as befitting the occasion. "Make your sneak like I told you, when they're so busy they haven't time to look your way. Take no chances of being seen. There's lots of time. If you *are* diskivered before you get there, pull out. Don't linger. Get away. We'll just let that part of it go then. Ef'n you get caught hauling at the wagons, drop flat and put up a fight. Hold 'em off best you can. It won't be for long; we'll be with you in two shakes. Ef'n you get a hole made all right without no one seeing you, hop into a wagon and lie flat. Don't you try to get in no fight afoot. We'll tend to the fight part of it. As soon as we charge in, *you get out,* as fast as you can. No ifs and ands. Understand?" There was fire in Andy's eyes.

"Yes, *señor padre*," said Djo, standing very erect.

"Well, you better; I'm serious." The fire slowly died. "If you behave yourselves and do this right there ought not to be much danger. We'll be watching, and we'll hop in *pronto* if it looks like it's necessary. But I don't want to git any of you boys hurt less'n it's necessary. That"—he turned to Means—"is another reason I'm sending you. Djo's the boss because he knows more about this kind of game, but I'm lookin' to you just the same. That's all. Git along with you and get hid before it gets too light."

He took it entirely for granted that Leslie was to be included in this singular warfare; nor did it occur to the young man that his official and sworn position under the government might be inconsistent with his taking a part. But if it had, it is doubtful if the thought would have influenced him. Shortly he and Djo and Abel Means and the two slim *californio* youths set off in the darkness. Djo carried the rifle he had brought from Monterey and wore his long throwing knife; Abel Means had likewise a rifle and a pair of single-shot horse pistols; Leslie had his Colt's and his derringer and in addition was given a light-calibered short-stocked rifle that Djo said had been especially made for him as a boy.

"It's too small and light, really," said he, "but it might help. It's all there is."

2

Soon after daylight the first band of cattle moved. To Leslie, concealed with his companions in the high yellow mustard on the sidehill below the ring of wagons, it was a wonderful sight. They came in a long narrow brown river, crowding between the hills and the deep ditch that stood to the grainfields in lieu of a fence. Once below that restriction, they spread across the whole width of the valley. Then for the first time the riders became intermittently visible through the thin haze of dust, darting back and forth at full speed, on their task of getting this unwieldy mass into rapid motion. At first so heavy was the impression of inertia, this seemed to Leslie impossible. But the *vaqueros* were masters of beasts. They swung their *reatas;* they dashed into the milling mass, leaning from their saddles to play their quirts or to twist tails. But especially they gave voice to queer sharp cries that seemed to have a maddening effect, not only on the cattle, but upon their own mounts as well. The brown flood heaved sluggishly forward, suddenly broke, as a dam breaks to pressure of water.

Even to Leslie, safely above level on the sidehill, the sight of this rushing torrent of beasts was stupendous in its feeling of the irresistible, for it seemed that no physical structure could stand against it and no physical power could stem or deflect it from its course. Remembering his introduction to these acres of Folded Hills, he could see with the eyes of those in the path of this living avalanche. He shivered with a vicarious thrill.

The oval enclosed by the wagons seethed into activity. Evidently aroused by the bawling and the dust of the herd when slowly approaching down the lane between the ditch and the hill, the squatters were already out and afoot. Some climbed for a moment to the wagon boxes in order better to see. But the majority, after a brief glance of identification, had gone about their affairs of beginning the day. The business of rodeo interested them little. Even with the first urgings of the riders comprehension had failed to come. A few—and among them, Leslie suspected, were the three Indian fighters—had climbed to wagon seats for a better view. Only after the cattle had definitely broken did someone appear to understand. Leslie could see him waving his arms, clamoring for attention, and the arrested attitudes of those who had been moving about on the morning's errands. The man pointed, shouted something. Leslie was too far away to hear the words. But the wagon corral broke into beelike activity. Men darted to wagons, probably in search of weapons, returned with rifles in their hands, urged vigorously forward by the man on the wagon box, and dropped on their bellies beneath the wagons. Women and older girls scurried about more frantically, collecting children, hoisting them into the wagon boxes. Leslie recognized instantly that here must be a complication when it came time for him and his companions to attempt to move some of the wagons. He glanced at Djo. Djo's brows were knit. Evidently the thought had occurred to him also. But Leslie had no time to worry about that now. Things were happening. Rifles were cracking, their sharp reports the only sounds audible above the rush of the cattle. A beast—another—another stumbled, went down, disappeared beneath the brown flood. The front rank wavered, tried to turn to right and left, were swept on by the press of those behind, half sidewise, still struggling mightily, leaning the whole weights of their bodies in a frantic effort to change their direction. In this they succeeded at last, though a few, unable to hold their feet against the current, were swept sidewise to collide with a resounding crash against the wagons themselves. The vehicles shook but were too wide and solid to be so easily overset by a single impact. Nevertheless Leslie could well imagine the leap of heart each of these collisions must cause to those on a level with the imminent flood, and he almost found it in him to sympathize with the frantic haste of the reloading.

Then with a roar the herd had swept by on either side.

The pursuing riders, following their orders, had magically disappeared to right and left into the hills. A slow following billow of dust rolled lazily across the encampment, half obscuring it, settled almost as though with a sigh of completion.

Leslie turned to Djo. Djo was staring into space, two lines between his eyes.

"We'll make a try for that patch of sage on the next run," said he. "As far as I could see nobody paid any attention except to the cattle. Did you see anyone, Leslie?"

"I—I'm afraid I wasn't looking," Leslie stammered.

"The dust is going to help," said Djo appraisingly. "It will get thicker the more cattle are driven." He looked at Leslie. "What you shaking for? Scared?" he asked.

"I'm not scared," protested Leslie stoutly. "I'm just shivering. It's cold."

He felt Djo's eyes on him in detached appraisal. It was as though Djo were a stranger. He flushed again, indignant at himself, indignant that the sheer spectacle had blinded him to the elementary observations, indignant that mere excitement should so uncontrolledly unsteady his hands and body. He looked Djo squarely in the eye, almost with defiance. Djo stared back at him impersonally, as though in judgment.

"All right," said Djo finally, "I know how it is. I was that way first time I was waiting to shoot a bear. You get over it when there's something to do. It's just the waiting."

The warmth of self-esteem returned to Leslie's veins at this understanding. And curiously enough the shaking stopped.

"What about those women and children in the wagons?" he asked. "They're going to bother us, aren't they? They'll give us away. How are we going to take care of them?"

"There's none in the wagon with the yellow wheels or the one next it on the left," said Djo briefly.

Leslie again subsided to his own disesteem. He had not noticed that.

"Here comes another batch," said Djo. He spoke to the Californian youths. "Now, all of you," he warned, "don't watch down there this time. Watch me. Do as I do. We'll make a try to get nearer."

3

With each successive wave of cattle driven down the valley, the dust clouds rose thicker as the turf was torn and the soil pulverized. With each successive wave the emulative excitement of the young *californios* and their *vaqueros* arose to higher and higher pitch. From their point of view the thing was succeeding beyond expectation. The Missourians were thoroughly bamboozled by the demonstration. They shot desperately and as rapidly as they could reload. There was no doubt that, with each splitting of the herd, the defenders drew deep breaths of relief over a destruction but just averted. To the light-spirited *californios,* who knew that the same thing would have taken place without a shot fired, this was a huge and private joke. The situation became farcical to them. They skylarked. Under cover of the dust cloud one of the riders dashed fairly up against the wagons, whirling the loop of his *reata*. No living mark presented itself for his cast. He contented himself with snatching from its socket on a wagon's footboard a long-lashed "bull" whip, which he dragged away after him as he fled, laughing derisively. The rifles were empty, but a scatter of pistol bullets whistled by him harmlessly.

His example was contagious. As nothing small and movable remained to snare as a trophy, the young riders swooped past to strike the canvas covers of the wagons resounding blows with their extended *reatas*. It became a game, for a time played without accident. The billowing clouds of dust rolling along after the herds were so thick that the horsemen were able to dash in and to dash out again so quickly and from such unexpected angles that none of them were hit. Andy from his hilltop could not see what was going on. Then the dust cleared to discover one horse down and its rider, by the grace of the blessed saints, loping away ahold of another's stirrup leather, and a second horse limping painfully from the field, its rider swaying in his saddle, clinging desperately to his pommel. Two riders, already well on their way, discovering his plight, turned back to help. Rifles cracked. Another horse went down. One of the riders fell from his saddle heavily, like a sack of grain. Others rode down the hill to the rescue. The wounded man and the dead man were somehow carried off. The two dead horses remained on the field.

Andy, seeing these things from his vantage place, was furiously angry. He mounted his horse behind the shelter of the hills and dashed to the head of the valley where awaited in eager impatience those in charge of the bands of cattle yet to make the run. These he lashed to sobriety, threatening to shoot with his own rifle any who departed from the strict business of the occasion. Panchito, who had tried in vain to hold down their exuberance, looked grimly triumphant. Andy returned to his lookout. The operations had been interrupted for nearly an hour. The cattle were milling restlessly, for they were thirsty with the strengthening sun.

The last hour had had other effects on the situation. The *californios* gathered behind the hill were angry. The *fiesta* mood had evaporated. This was no longer a lark. The killing of the young Cermenos and the horses and the wounding of Basil Constansio had driven home the realities. It is probable that most of those present appreciated that reality for the first time: that these people below them, on the flat, within the circle of wagons, were not playing a part in a rather entertaining drama; that they were there in serious intention as despoilers; that the outrage of appropriation and destruction begun was not part of *opéra bouffe,* over with the fall of curtain, but something accomplished and actual that might next happen to each and any one of them. Their handsome faces set grimly. They dismounted and thoughtfully drew on the broad *látigos,* tightening the *cinchas* of their saddles, and that, with these horsemen, was significant as a symbol of determination.

This Andy, riding up, noted with satisfaction. But the satisfaction was mixed. He drew Ramon aside.

"I'm talking to you seriously, *valedor,*" said he. "This is no time for jesting."

"That I understand," said Ramon.

Andy looked at his friend's face that had sobered to attention.

"Those skylarking fools have done a heap of damage," said he, shifting to English. "I'd thought we could rush the wagons sometime when I figgered they'd emptied all their rifles. They won't do that now."

"No?" Ramon looked his inquiry.

"No. They'll be holding their fire—some of it—for more of these crazy loons."

"I see," said Ramon.

"And that," said Andy, "means somebody's going to git hurt. No way out. These can shoot." He shook his head. "We're bound to lose men. I hoped maybe we wouldn't have to. What I want to know is: can we sit down and starve 'em out?"

"No," said Ramon promptly.

"That's what I figgered." Andy looked at the frowning intent faces about him, sighed. "Your people are good fighters, Ramon, and that's what I always said, but they only fight good while they're mad." He drew his long figure erect and stretched his hands above his head. "Well," said he, "we'll go at it. But we got no time now to monkey. We'll throw all we got at them at once and do our best. If we dribble along as we been doing they'll soon get onto the fact that the cattle won't run over 'em." He thrust his head cautiously above the grass level to appraise the situation below. "They've knocked over a dozen critters already," said he. "Pile up a few more and we'll have trouble driving down the valley at all. All right. You ride up and bring down every head of beef that's left up there. Start 'em fast and keep 'em coming. See if you can't make 'em think hell's at their tails." He turned his gray eyes mildly on his friend. "When," he drawled in exaggerated trapper lingo, "you git the critters past, ef'n you see anything of a fight goin' on, you might pile in: it's likely to be a good one!"

"How about Djo?" asked Ramon. "He's not at the wagons yet."

"No," said Andy, "that's why I'm so mad at these damn fools that started this. Wish I'd seen 'em! However"—he hunched his shoulders, shrugging that off—"soon's I see your dust close enough, I'll start 'em off. They got to take a chance." His brows were knit with a real anxiety. If the lad and his companions started too soon and should be seen by anybody within the wagon circle, they could hardly escape the squatters' rifles. If, on the other hand, the rush of cattle caught them before they had traversed the flat to the shelter of the wagons, they must be trampled underfoot. Ramon also saw this point.

"No"—Andy negatived his suggestion—"won't do. See what happens: by the time mounted men could hop off'n their hosses and pull away the wagons to make a hole through you'd have them shooting right in the thick of you, and yo're all huddled together at that. We'd lose half our men, or more. We're agoin' to lose consid'able as it is." He fell silent, pondering. Confident as he was— as he had always been—of the basic courage of the Californians, he could not but admit to himself that to attack expert riflemen practically barehanded required something approaching fanaticism. Would they carry through when this fact was borne in on them by the actual test? Not unless the planned surprise worked out; that was certain. Aloud he said, "I've changed my mind about one thing. Don't you bother about any fight that's goin' on. Let your *vaqueros* take care of that. This is your job, and Panchito's; you look for Djo and his lot, and you stand ready to snake them up behind you and *git out* with 'em if things look like they're—well, like they mout be goin' wrong. Understand?"

Ramon nodded.

"They's five of 'em. You and Panchito, and you'll need three more. Pick your men well, and see that they stick to just that and nothin' else. I'm dependin' on you. I won't have time to bother myself, and anyway, you'll be comin' along, behind the cattle, just about the right time."

"Djo will not come," suggested Ramon.

"He's had his marching orders, but I'm going to sneak down to where he is and give them to him all over again," said Andy grimly. "He'll come! This thing ain't going to be decided by two-three rifles. It'll be the *reata,* and cold iron—or nothin'." He patted Ramon on the shoulder. "All right; git agoin'. You wait up there where you can see. I'll wave my hat when to start."

Ramon mounted, flashed his white teeth in his old gay smile.

"Be not escare, *valedor!*" he cried. "I shall r-remove Djo myself. Is he not my *ahijado*—what you call?—my godson? If he shall not come, then I may—I may—what you call?—espank!"

4

After fifteen minutes had passed the men lying under the wagons arose.

"Reckon that's got 'em licked," they said on varying notes of satisfaction and doubt.

Stampede

"We sure got meat for a barbecue!" chuckled one of the younger men.

"Reckon they're through, Williams?" queried someone from one of the Indian fighters.

"Sartin!" returned the latter contemptuously. "Kill one or two of 'em and they quit like dogs. I fit 'em under Taylor."

"Those were Mexs," observed a graybeard on a tone of doubt.

"Greaser's greasers," returned Williams succinctly. "Sometimes they put up quite a argument for a while, but once you got 'em licked, they stay licked."

A man perched on a wagon box spat copiously into the powdery dust outside.

"Then I reckon we ain't got 'em licked," he observed dryly, "fer it looks like to me they's a lot more where they come from!"

They crowded to the wagons to look up the valley.

"It's shore a lot of dust," said someone. "Reckon they're comin' agin?"

"I bet you they air!" The man on the wagon glared contemptuously at Ransom. "Thought you said as how these greasers wouldn't fight?"

"Well, they haven't fit, have they?" demanded Ransom

belligerently. "Do you call it fightin', drivin' a lot of dumb beasts?"

"Mebbe it's not fightin'," said the graybeard, "but it kept my bar'l hot. Looked to me like we just about saved our ha'r, whatever you call it."

"Keep this up, we're li'ble to set around here till Fourth er July!" grumbled the misanthrope on the wagon box.

"They won't keep it up," said Ransom confidently.

"You said they wouldn't fight," the other pointed out. "Looks to me like they done put up a purty good job."

"Hell!" said Ransom in disgust. "What's the matter with you! Gittin' yaller? Expect things handed to you on a silver platter?" He looked about him for approval. The tall, sallow man nodded gravely. Thus encouraged, Ransom went on. "Got yore land, ain't ye? And dang good land. And if it warn't for this renegade white man——" He stopped, checked by a sudden shift in the group about him. A powerfully built man with a full seal brown beard thrust himself forward.

"What's this about a white man?" he demanded. "You didn't tell us about no white man."

"There wa'n't nothing to tell, Porter," protested Ransom stoutly, but evidently on the defensive. "He's just one of these renegades, turned greaser years ago."

Stampede 215

"What's he got to do with it?" persisted Porter. "Where does he come in?"

"Well, he's supposed to own this ranch," admitted Ransom reluctantly.

The big man ripped out an oath.

"I never aimed to have no truck with ary white man's land," said he.

"But this feller's no white man," insisted Ransom. "You saw him. He's gone greaser as yaller as the best on 'em."

"Elmer! Hi, you, Elmer!" called a shrill voice. A woman's sunbonnet protruded from the puckered cover of a wagon. "Kain't we all git down?"

"You stay whar you be till I tell you," replied the big man decisively.

"But the children got to git down——"

"You heerd me!" Porter shut her up. He turned to Ransom. "Greaser or no greaser, he's a white man, and it's a white man we're fightin'."

"I didn't know you were so plumb sentimental on white men," sneered Ransom.

The other stared him down contemptuously.

"When you fight a white man," he condescended at last, "you ain't fightin' a fool greaser with only one idee in his head. Yere you, Tawm: you sneak over and watch out in the rear thar that nobody attacks thar, and Jake and Jimmy watch out both sides. Crawl around clost under the wagons so nobody sees you take yore places. I've fit greasers in Mexico," he muttered quaintly in his beard, "and I've fit Injuns, and I kind of trust 'em, but I don't trust no white man."

"Gee-ker snipes!" exclaimed the man on the wagon box. "Look at that!"

He extended his arm up the valley. In the distance a brown mass was pouring slowly over the summit of the hill and down the slope, like a sluggish, muddy river. Across the face of it sharp eyes could just make out the mounted figures riding back and forth, holding control until Ramon should receive the signal.

"There must be a million of 'em!" said the lookout, awed.

"They're goin' to make their big try this time," said Porter. "Stand steady, boys, and shoot clost."

"Do we shoot this time?" asked one of the men.

"No," said Porter.

"They's a power of 'em," said the man, glancing doubtfully up the valley. "Do you-all think you can turn 'em?"

"Ef'n we don't, I'll let you know," said Porter with

a certain grim humor. "You hold yore fire. And," he added, "you keep yore eye on Tawm and Jake and Jimmy and you let me know ef'n anything comes up."

"What you thinkin', Cap?" asked another curiously.

"Nothin'," admitted Porter, "exceptin' I don't trust no white man, and I ain't intendin' anybody's goin' to sneak in on us without gittin' a bellyful of lead."

5

Andy, unaware of this new development, paused for a last look around before giving the signal which would launch Ramon and his men on their wild charge. Djo and his companions he had visited. They had reached the last patch of cover safely above the flat. It was over a hundred yards from the wagons. This hundred yards they must traverse. They must do so only after the cattle had been stampeded near enough to hold the attention of the squatters. Naturally they must complete the distance before the leaders could trample them. It was a nice calculation at best. They knew nothing of Tawm and Jake and Jimmy and the almost certain death of the long rifle barrels now protruding between the spokes of wheels. Andy had made the journey to and from Djo's concealment unseen. He was satisfied Djo understood what he must do and that he intended to obey the injunction to keep out of the fight.

Behind the concealment of the hills to which he returned awaited the riders who had already made the runs, some forty-odd in number. Probably twice that number remained with Ramon. Here also were some of the older men, including Don Sylvestro himself. A few carried big smooth bore pistols at their saddlebows; a few had lances taken from the walls where they had hung for many years; a few even sported slim old-fashioned rapiers. But all carried knives and the deadly *reata*. They were grimly in earnest. Andy believed they would stick. He had only one word for them.

"Don't fight them any more than you must, señores," said he. "Rope them and tie them up. Work fast before they can recharge their pieces."

They nodded, balancing their rawhide loops.

The sun was by now near the meridian. The breeze that blew every afternoon up the valley from the sea was beginning faintly to stir. It bore with it certain small homely sounds from the *rancho*, sounds such as the slow contemplative clucking of hens that stood out daintily in relief against their background of the dull and heavy

Stampede 219

bawling of the cattle. For a queer instant the eternal quietudes that were made up of just these small accustomed things, and the sunshine, and the mountains, and the serene detachment of birds alone seemed real to Andy, and all this dust and row of danger and death were illusory as mist. He laughed and snapped back. They were genuine enough. He straightened in his saddle, took off his broad hat to wave the signal to Ramon.

XIII

PEDRO, the *mozo,* who had been left on watch, slipped through the tall mustard on the hilltop.

"Señor!" he gasped. "One comes!"

"One comes where? What?" Andy was impatient, but he stayed his signal, impressed by the man's excitement.

"Down the middle of the valley—where the cattle run—from the direction of the *casa*—in plain view!"

"Well, what of it?"

"But this one has the look of an *hidalgo,* señor!"

"Who is it? Do you know him?"

"No, señor."

Andy slipped from his saddle and dropped the reins over his horse's head. The degree of the man's excitement was inexplicable, even though this stranger were blundering into real danger. Andy ducked through the mustard to a point of vantage.

Down the middle of the valley, as Pedro had said, rode at a foot pace a stranger. He was headed directly toward the wagons. The animal he rode was a fine one, finely caparisoned in the Californian manner. The rider was not a Californian; nor was he dressed in any fashion familiar to Andy. He wore a high beaver hat, a light blue tailed coat, tight pantaloons strapped under the insteps of thin varnished boots, gloves of light lemon color. In his hand he carried, at what even the untutored Andy knew instinctively to be the correct angle, a short-knobbed riding crop, an implement also unfamiliar. He sat his horse well and gracefully, with the ease of the accomplished rider.

Apparently his whole interest was centered in the pleasure of his ride. He seemed to be unaware of the menace or the existence of the wagons, to which by now he had drawn near, incurious of the dead cattle at which his horse shied aside daintily. His eyes rested on the vivid yellow green of the new foliage on the oaks, were attracted upward by the shadow of a vulture. He struck idly at the top of an artemisia. He seemed not to hear hoarse commands to halt; nor did he pay attention to the rifle barrels thrust forward in threat from beneath the cover of the wagons. Only when his horse stopped, its nose fairly against a wheel, did the stranger appear to come to himself. Andy saw him lean forward slightly in his saddle. Apparently he held a short colloquy with those inside the corral of wagons. Then he lifted his reins. The horse half reared, executed a pretty turn—the demivolte of the riding schools, had Andy known anything about riding schools. The extraordinary stranger then rode slowly and serenely up the hill through the tall yellow mustard, directly toward Andy's concealment.

2

Andy slipped back over the brow of the hill. He had no wish that the stranger should stumble upon him in the grass and so disclose his presence, and time pressed for the delivery of the attack. But as though the horseman had sensed his withdrawal, he put his animal to a canter up the slope. So he overtook Andy as the latter reached his own horse and the waiting group of *californios*. He reined in, raised his riding crop in easy and negligent

Stampede

salute, ignoring the stares of astonishment that greeted his appearance.

"Mr. Burnett," he stated rather than inquired. Andy felt himself the object of a scrutiny that checked him with a quality he could not define. He nodded shortly.

"I'll talk to you later," said he. "I have business afoot."

"So," said the stranger, "I perceive. It is of that business I wish to speak."

"What is it of yours?" demanded Andy.

"None, none whatever," admitted the stranger.

"Then stand one side," said Andy. A sudden thought struck him. "How did you know where to find me?"

"I inquired of your charming wife."

"She told you? You have been to the *casa!*" cried Andy, his face darkening. He remembered the stranger's pause at the wagons. "What is your business here?" he demanded bluntly.

"I have no interest whatever in the trespassers on your land," said the stranger as though reading his thoughts, "nor have I disclosed aught to them. And Mrs. Burnett was justified in accepting my assurances of good faith." He was smiling quizzically, surveying Andy's perplexity with a delighted mischief. For Andy was indeed perplexed.

If the man were lying, if he had passed on to the defenders of the wagons the fact that over this hill lay a flanking force ready to attack, why then all this careful strategy was useless. And if the attack were launched, if Djo and his little party were to attempt to cross the open space that lay before them, they must be annihilated. Of course the man might be sincere; how did it happen that Carmel had confided in him so readily? Carmel had more sense. Dared he take that chance?

"I think you must tell me what your business is here. And quickly," said he.

The *californios* moved restlessly. They did not understand the stranger's presence, nor the purport of this long colloquy.

"*Que es, señor?*" they asked.

Andy silenced them with a gesture.

"What are you doing here?" he demanded roughly.

The stranger produced a long cheroot, the end of which he clipped with a penknife. He prolonged the operation with a hidden enjoyment that at the same time both perplexed and angered Andy.

"Speak up!" he urged. His straight brows were drawn together dangerously. The stranger examined him and laughed lightly.

"Perhaps I'd better," said he. "I was at Monterey. I heard rumor of squatter trouble up the valley." He spoke now crisply and to the point. "If there was trouble anywhere in his vicinity I knew my nephew would be in the thick of it. So here I am! Where is my nephew? That is my business here."

Ramon dashed up at full speed, scattering turf and pebbles fanwise before his horse's forefeet as he wrenched the animal to its haunches.

"*Valedor*," he cried, "what is wrong? We cannot much longer hold the cattle. They thirst. They will break from us!"

"Wait," said Andy in English, raising the flat of his hand toward Ramon, but keeping his eyes keenly on the other. "This man is Leslie's uncle. I will tell you where your nephew is," said he. "He is with my son and three others on the edge of the brush just this side of the wagons. When my friend here drives those cattle against the wagons, these boys are goin' to make a dash across and pull out a wagon or so to make a hole for me and these others to git in through. That," said he deliberately, "sounds dangersome, but it's purty safe." His eyes bored into the depths of the other's. Now, said Andy to himself, if he's said ary word to the squatters, he must show it, for that would mean certain death to his kin. Apparently he was satisfied, for after a tense half-minute he turned to Ramon.

"All right, Ramon," said he, "let 'em come through."

"Wait!" commanded the stranger with a snap of authority in his voice. "I think, if you will give me a chance, I can resolve this matter."

"It ain't a matter for argument," said Andy. "These men have got to get off my land."

"I'll get 'em off."

"You!" Andy stared at him. "What makes you think you can do that?" His eyes were narrowed with returning suspicion.

"Give me an hour."

"I ain't got an hour," said Andy bluntly. "I can't hold my cattle—or my men—that long." A thought struck him that softened the lines between his eyes. "I'll send Pedro down to order Leslie to keep out of this," said he.

The other thrust this aside with an impatient gesture.

"He can take a chance as well as your son," said he.

Andy frowned at him from beneath lowered brows, all his suspicions returning. How did he even know the man was Leslie's uncle, as he claimed? Something funny about this. The whole affair was suspicious. Why had he stopped at the wagons? Andy for once was undecided. He did not know what to do; what he dared do. He studied the man's face. He liked it. And about it there was something hauntingly familiar, something that plucked at his memory. About the man's lips came and went a mysterious smile, as though of a secret amusement.

"*Amigo,*" pleaded Ramon.

The stranger's smile deepened.

"I think I'd have known you anyway, Andy," said he. "You've changed, of course, but those eyebrows I could not mistake. And is that the same rifle? The rifle that old Dan'l Boone carried?" He leaned from his saddle to touch the stock of the weapon with his forefinger. He looked up into Andy's straight stare, his own eyes surprisingly misted. "Don't you know me, Andy?" he pleaded. Andy continued to stare, recollection slowly piecing itself in the back of his brain. His mind moved slowly back and forth, groping through crowded years. His eyes widened.

"Russ Braidwood!" he gasped. He reached from his saddle to envelop the other man's shoulder in his mighty grasp. "My God, man, where did you come from? Where have you been?"

3

Ramon thrust his mount forward insistently.

"Andreo!" he pleaded, "what are we to do? We cannot hold the cattle longer! Look how they are breaking for the water!"

"Haste, Don Largo!" "Give the signal." "We lose the chance," urged others.

Andy turned to them a shining countenance.

"Señores," said he, the words poured out from him in unaccustomed and breathless haste, "here, by the grace of the blessed saints, comes the only friend I knew as a boy. It is thirty years since I have seen him. Why, he and I"—Andy chuckled affectionately—"the first day we laid eyes on each other, fought over nothing until we fell down in an icy puddle, and so became fast friends. He knew my old home—he himself lived near there. He knew my grandmother. It was because of him, in a way, that I left my home. Do you understand Spanish?" he asked of Braidwood.

"A little. I understand what you are saying."

"Señor," Don Sylvestro spoke up with formality, "it is gratifying to us that you have thus encountered an old friend, but it is still a fact that Ramon awaits your commands."

Andy looked at Braidwood inquiringly.

"You said an hour?" he asked. At Braidwood's nod the *ranchero* turned again to the Californians. "My friend thinks it possible he may be able to arrange matters. We shall give him the chance."

"I cannot hold the cattle. We lose our chance," said Ramon.

"Let them water; there is always *mañana*," said Andy. In the word he voiced the philosophy of the race; yet the *californios* looked sullen or rebellious, and Ramon rode away, shaking his head.

4

Braidwood descended the hill through the mustard. Djo and his companions watched him with curiosity. As he debouched from the high growth to plain view, Leslie uttered an exclamation. Djo caught his expression of blank amazement.

"It's my uncle!" gasped Leslie.

"Your uncle! What's he doing here?"

"I don't know."

"What business has he with these robbers?"

"I don't know!" Leslie half started up as though to show himself to the horseman.

"Sit tight!" commanded Djo, hauling him down none too gently.

XIV

BRAIDWOOD stopped his horse ten feet from the wagons.

"Ransom," he challenged in his high, clear voice, "what have you been telling these people?"

For a moment no one spoke. It was Powers, of the square seal-brown beard, who finally replied.

"Who air you that yore questions should be answered?" he demanded.

"Ask Ransom if he knows me," returned Braidwood crisply. "That is," he added, "if you still believe what he says."

Powers turned his head.

"Ransom," he called. "Whar be ye, Ransom?"

No one replied.

"He was right yere by me a few minutes ago," said one of the younger men.

The question of Ransom's whereabouts was instantly resolved. From diagonally across the wagon circle came the sounds of a violent scuffle. Appeared Tawm prodding the reluctant Ransom forward with the muzzle of his rifle.

"I'd moved over from whar I was lying to git me a gourd of water," explained Tawm, "and I cotched him just drawing a bead on this yere stranger. I didn't know whether you wanted the stranger kilt or not, so I kicked up his shootin' iron and brung him along over. Did you want him kilt?"

"Ef'n we want him kilt, we'll do it ourselves," returned the captain gravely. "You done right, Tawm. Git back to yore post, and keep yore eyes skinned." He turned to Ransom. "Wal, Ransom, speak up. What's the idee?"

"I'll tell you," interposed Braidwood. "The idea is that I know too much to suit him." He leveled a forefinger, like a pistol, at Ransom as the latter opened his mouth to bluster. "You're at the wrong tree, Ransom," he snapped. "You can't make this stick."

Stampede

"No?" Ransom found his voice. "What do you know about it? This title is——"

"Did he tell you that you are squatting on a white man's land?" Braidwood demanded of Powers, adopting the arrogant classification of the "conquerors."

Powers shook his head with a certain rueful humor.

"If we'd knowed that we never would have come," he acknowledged. "But," he added, "now we're here, I reckon we'll stay." The bystanders uttered a growl of approval.

"The man's a renegade," broke in Ransom, "a bastard yallerbelly. He's a white man turned greaser, and they ain't nothing more de-spisable than that, less'n it's a rattlesnake. And if I get a chance I'll tell him so, the——" And Ransom added other and more varied descriptions. "He ain't got no more right to hog the land than any other goddamn greaser!" He was feeling the sure ground of demagoguery beneath his feet and swept on in the specious and oratorical sophistry of the land-grabber, more for the benefit of the immigrants than for any effect on Braidwood. The latter allowed him to finish, an amused half-smile on his lips.

"Yes, that's the talk," he applauded when Ransom had had his say. "It generally sticks. But it won't stick here. You wish to know why? I could give you several reasons.

I'll give you two. The first is that Jake Conger will see that it doesn't."

"Jake Conger!" echoed Ransom on a slight accent of incredulous dismay.

"You doubt that?" Braidwood laughed shortly. "The Inspector at present examining this land—who is, by the way, my nephew—was appointed at Jake Conger's request. If you do not believe that now, you will find it out later."

"I didn't know Jake Conger was int'rested in this land," muttered Ransom, obviously taken aback.

"You should better inform yourself before your undertakings," said Braidwood sweetly. "What has this man told you?" he demanded again of Porter. Ransom recovered from his momentary dismay.

"I told him what everybody knows," he began aggressively. The man with the square beard stopped him peremptorily. "Light from yore hoss, stranger," he invited. "Looks like this will b'ar talkin' of."

2

Braidwood sat leaning against the wheel of a wagon, his horse's reins in his hand. The captain of the immigrants squatted to face him. The other men, with the exception of Tawm and his two fellow sentries, who stuck to their posts but cast longing eyes at the conclave, drew close.

"What, exactly, did this man tell you?" Braidwood repeated his question for the third time.

"Why, that this yere land was part and passel of one of these old grants that was no good."

"I see. How did he get you to come so far down country? There's plenty of land of the same kind nearer the city."

"That's tuk up. We're law-abiding citizens. We ain't no squatters. That there land ain't open no longer: it's all been took up—or declared reg'lar."

"And this was not regular and was open for entry. That right? Well"—Braidwood turned deliberately to confront Ransom—"he lied to you."

"Set still!" thundered Porter at Ransom's demonstration. "You subside! You'll have your turn. Zeke, you see he keeps quiet. I want to know more of this. Whar do you come in on this, stranger? How come you know so much?"

"I am associated with Jake Conger," said Braidwood simply. "You do not know who he is? Ask your friend Ransom. He'll tell you."

Porter glanced at Ransom, back at Braidwood, studying each from beneath shaggy brows.

"Explain yoreself," he grunted.

"Gladly, and briefly. This man makes a business of settling immigrants on land. It is but rarely that that land is actually open for settlement. But he makes it stick because he is in cahoots with political powers. In this case it happens that those political powers are on the other side of the fence. Is that clear?"

"I hear you say it," returned Porter guardedly. "What you got to say?" he asked Ransom.

Ransom had plenty to say in general denial and somewhat involved rebuttal. His appeal was, naturally, emotional.

"May I ask a question?" requested Braidwood, when he had finished.

"Speak up."

"Why did this man try to shoot me just now? So I would not tell you exactly what I am telling you." He answered his own question.

But Ransom pounced on his chance here.

"Hell!" he lied contemptuously. "I tried to kill you—and I'll kill you yet when I get a chanct—because you had the goddamn gall to fool with my gal, and you know it!"

Some of the younger men laughed. The reaction was decidedly in Ransom's favor. Some cried out impatiently for an end to this futile conference. The man with the seal-brown beard quieted them.

"Wait a minute." He turned to Braidwood. "What you trying to do, stranger? You ain't answered my question: whar do you come in? And what you aimin' to do?"

"I'm trying to avoid trouble," said Braidwood desperately, for he perceived the tide was setting against him. He turned to Ransom. "You aren't going to make this stick, you know. Until this title is decided to be bad, these people are squatters, nothing more, and are subject to ejectment as trespassers. You and your like have been able to quash ejectments on the Peralta lands, to be sure; but, as I told you, Jake Conger is interested in this case. You know what that means. There'll be troops down here, if necessary, to make the ejectment stick."

"So you say!" sneered Ransom for the benefit of the immigrants, but Braidwood saw plainly enough his concealed uneasiness. And, indeed, the man was already casting about in his mind for expedients by which he could, even without expected profits, drop out of a situation that he foresaw was going to be too hot to hold. In the meantime he must make good his temporary position. "Hell!"

he cried contemptuously. "Can't you see this feller's a spy?" He caught the stir of attention from the tall Missourians lounging against the wagon bodies. "He's holdin' us in talk while his friend, the *renegado*————"

"Hesh, you!" commanded Porter. He turned sternly on Braidwood. "Declar' yoreself, stranger. Jist what are you after? What you yere for? What you want us to do?"

Braidwood looked about him, appraising the sullen faces bent for his reply. His heart sank, for he sensed that he was in the presence of an ignorance and obstinacy impervious to the type of argument his civilized mind had thought to be compelling.

"I came here," nevertheless he said, "in the hope that a plain statement of fact would bring you to a realization of your position. You have been lied to by this man on every point, and you've followed him with your eyes shut, like a pack of fools. Why," he said stingingly, in defiance of the growl of resentment at this, "you didn't even know whose land you were claiming! You said so yourselves. You didn't even know he was a white man! You so confessed!" He arose, deliberately flicked away the soil from his pantaloons with his handkerchief.

"You going to let him git back and tell what he's spied?" cried Ransom. He tugged at a pistol but was restrained from using it by Zeke, who, nevertheless, looked inquiringly toward his chief for orders.

"That's right!" "Tie the son of a bitch up." "String him up where his friends can see him!" "Shoot him and have done with it!" One of the tall young men leaped agilely from the wagon box and seized Braidwood by the arm. "That's the stuff! Grab him!" yelped Ransom.

Braidwood did not struggle; nor did he appear to notice the surge forward of the younger men. He addressed himself directly to Porter. His voice was calm, his manner unruffled.

"I was allowed to come here freely," said he. "Am I not to be allowed to go as freely? Is that fair play? What should I spy on?"

"Let him go," said Porter curtly. "Let him go, I say!" he roared as the man appeared to hesitate.

Braidwood mounted, lifted his beaver hat.

"I will bid you good day, gentlemen," said he. "I assure you, in spite of Mr. Ransom's perhaps not unnatural suspicions, I am but this hour arrived. My errand has been voluntary, and my visit to you has been in the hope of rendering service to both parties. I shall, however, report to Mr. Burnett that my errand has been in vain. And, gentlemen"—his voice was cutting—"I do not conceal from you that, though until now I have been neutral, I shall align myself with his cause. Unless, of course," he added suavely, his head high, his eyes glittering, "you elect to shoot me in the back. That is your privilege."

"I reckon you'll not need to worry about that," said the man with the brown beard with a quiet gleam of humor. "We don't shoot in the back—especially men with your guts."

"I thank you," said Braidwood, and executed again the same riding-school half turn as before. But before he could ride away he was arrested by an abrupt command from Williams, the old Indian fighter, who had, throughout all the proceeding, sat back against a wagon wheel, his heavy buffalo rifle across his lap, placidly chewing tobacco.

"Wait a minute, you!" said Williams.

The horse reared, half turned, came down on its front feet, again facing the wagons.

"Well?" its rider demanded.

"What's that name you spoke?" asked Williams. "Burnett?"

"The man who owns this land. Do you mean to say you don't even know the name of the man you're trying to rob?" said Braidwood with contemptuous amazement.

"I know, but what's the rest of the name?" Williams brushed this aside.

"Andrew. Andrew Burnett," replied Braidwood.

"What for a man is he? About six foot or more? And is he a homely kind of cuss with black eyebrows that go straight across?" Braidwood nodded. "He ain't, by chance, still carryin' an old-fashion long rifle looks like it was made for old Noah himself?" Williams turned to the man with the square beard. He appeared to be greatly amused. "Wal, Elmer," he drawled, "I dunno, but it looks like it to me. You know who it looks like we're buckin'?"

"No. Who?"

"I-tam-api," said Williams with relish.

"Sho! No!" cried Porter after a blank pause.

"Sounds like him," said Williams.

"Who's I-tam-api?" asked one of the younger men.

"Who's Kit Carson? Who's Jesus Christ?" Williams subdued this ignorance contemptuously.

Porter's face darkened with sudden passion. He turned upon Ransom.

"You mean to tell me you brung us all this way to put us down on land belonging to a man like I-tam-api? Why, you pore———"

"Wait a minute." Williams laid his hand on Porter's knee. "We ain't sartin, you know."

Porter heaved himself to his feet.

"Well, we're agoin' to *be* sartin," he growled. "You used to know him; come along. As for this pizen snake"—he turned upon the justifiably puzzled Ransom—"take his arms. Tie him up ef'n you have to. I want him yere when I come back. Now, stranger," he said to Braidwood, "lead us up to this Burnett. I want to see ef'n he is genuwine."

3

The two men trudged up through the mustard on either side of Braidwood's horse. To his tentative questions they opposed an obstinate silence. Over the brow of the hill Andy sat his horse, waiting. With him were the Californians, some of them mounted, most of them apart, squatted on their heels, their bridle reins in their hands, silent and somewhat sullen over this distasteful turn of affairs, for far up the valley the widening dust clouds attested the scattering of the herds. Djo was there, and Leslie and Abel Means and the two *californio* youths who had been with them, recalled by Andy as soon as he knew his position was no longer secret.

The three stopped at the crest of the hill.

"It's him," the old plainsman told his companion.

They moved forward again. Williams raised his right hand, palm forward.

"How, I-tam-api!" said he.

Andy's face betrayed a momentary surprise from which instantly he recovered. He raised his own right hand in similar gesture.

"How!" He returned the greeting. His eyes searched the other's countenance for recognition but failed. He waited composedly.

The big man stepped forward, planted his feet apart, spoke in his great voice.

"I'm yere to say that ef'n we'd known who you are, we wouldn't be yere. We been fooled. You won't be troubled no more. I kain't say fairer. Come on, Williams." He turned to go away as though his whole errand here were finished.

At the name Andy's face lighted in recollection. He slapped his hand so violently that his horse leaped, startled.

"Seth Williams, by the 'tarnal!" he cried. He spurred his mount sidewise to lean from the saddle in grasp of the other's hand. "I'd never know you! You've done changed! What you hiding your face for in all that brush?" His own face was beaming with an animation so foreign to its customary gravity that the *californios* stared in arrested astonishment. "My God, it's been a long time!"

"Rising thutty year," said Williams, his own face, even behind its "hiding of brush," shining with smiles.

"You old horny toad!" cried Andy.

The two men pumped at each other's arms, too engrossed with one another to notice for the moment that Porter had turned his back and was walking purposefully away again toward the valley.

"Hi there, stranger," Andy called after the square sturdy figure, "come back here! Whar you going?"

Porter faced about.

"Snake killin'," said he briefly and proceeded on his way.

Andy's horse leaped to the spur.

"Let be," he said, looking down from his saddle to Porter's upturned face. "We got to talk this over. He'll keep. No object going off half cock. We got to have a big smoke on all this."

"I shore despise a coyote," said Porter, his jaw set. He met Andy's eyes. "Ef'n you ask it, I-tam-api," he yielded reluctantly.

"I do," said Andy.

"All right," said Porter.

Andy leaned from the saddle to clap him on the shoulder.

"I better go tell my folks." Porter turned away again.

"And I better talk to mine," agreed Andy. "Tonight, come sundown. At the *casa*." He grinned. "I reckon we'll have beef enough for everybody," said he.

The immigrant's eyes turned to the valley below and the fringe of cattle carcasses across the wagons' fronts, and he, too, grinned.

"I reckon," said he.

"Looks like the war's over," observed Braidwood dryly to no one in particular.

"War!" spoke up Williams, almost indignantly. "Agin I-tam-api?"

XV

THE DUSK was falling. Russell Braidwood stood apart with his nephew, staring in silence at the spectacle before him. He could not rid himself of the impression that by some magic he had been transported to the old romantic past of days long gone. He had to shake his head and look about him with deliberately focused eyes to realize that this was indeed the present, the year of our Lord 1853, and that this was the land of California.

Beneath the spreading oak gleamed a tiny fire. Seated cross-legged about it were five men. They stared into the flames, listening while one of their number talked. The one who talked was on his feet. When he had finished, he sat down. Then whoever had anything to say, in his turn, arose. This had been going on for an hour. When first the five men had sat down, and before a word was spoken, Andy had produced a calumet, or Indian pipe. Its bowl was of stone and had come with him in his "possible" sack when he had crossed the Sierra from the plains country. He had fitted it with a long reed mouthpiece which he had decorated with feathers, so that now again it was as it had been back in its Indian origins. This he had stuffed with tobacco and ignited with a coal. When it was well going, he pointed with the stem to each of the four points of the compass, then toward the zenith, and downward toward the earth, after which he took from it three long whiffs and passed it to his neighbor. The latter likewise drew on it thrice and passed it on. When it had rounded the circle Andy arose to his feet and spoke the first words of the conference.

For a time Braidwood scarcely heard what was said, so fascinated was he by the mere spectacle. In the shadows outside the illumination of the fire many people stood motionless. In a somber group to one side were a dozen tall Missourians, apart, their faces stolid, holding together compactly, suspicious in spite of the explicit assurances of their leaders, uneasy that their protests had been overruled and they had come unarmed. The *californios,* in gay contrast of raiment, were scattered around the other segments of the circle; the *rancheros* and *hacendados* in two close groups about Djo and Ramon, who translated to them in low voices; the ranch people and visiting *vaqueros* at a more respectful distance, watching these strange proceedings with alert but unsatisfied curiosity. Of them could be seen, as the darkness gathered, only an occasional gleam of metal or of white, or some slight movement that stirred the shadows. The white background of the *casa* more clearly defined the women of the household: Carmel seated, her anxieties but partly allayed; Amata on one side, leaning against the back of the chair, her mother's hand in hers; old Vicenta on the other, holding her great bulk tirelessly and defiantly erect. This was a great multitude, for no human was absent from the gathering, and yet no sound or whisper broke the stillness of the evening save the slow-measured voices of the councilors at the fire and the faint murmur of Djo's and Ramon's whispered comments.

Braidwood's quick imagination was afire. He was no longer in the California that he knew. He was in a past of which at firsthand he could know nothing, in a scene his eyes had never beheld. It seemed to him that by the slightest shift of focus a hidden reality would clothe itself in its proper physical seeming, that this grave small group about the fire and the hushed multitude in the background might transform, so that in his own proper eyes he would be looking upon feathered and blanketed warriors. So imminent was the illusion that almost his senses persuaded him. The dim people, waiting darkened, reëmerged: painted tribesmen, cowled and muffled squaws, a gleam of tepees in the night. The soft evening breeze sharpened in the chill of a greater spaciousness.

His eyes caught Leslie's. They were shining. Braidwood seized his nephew's hand in a clasp of shared understanding.

The spell was broken by Djo at his elbow. Djo had for the moment left his self-imposed task of translation for other explanations. He was eager that his friends should miss nothing.

"It is a council fire," he said in guarded tones. "See how it is made? The sticks are all pointing away from a common center. And the pipe. Did you notice it passed from left to right around the circle? That means it is a real 'medicine smoke.' If it had been an 'ordinary smoke,' a 'friendship smoke,' it would have passed from right to left. They are all old Mountain Men—except the big man, Porter."

He glided away again.

"What about that, I-tam-api?" asked the speaker of the moment and sat down.

I-tam-api! There seemed to be in these syllables a grave and portentous respect, a magic that commanded. And it came to Braidwood that he heard in them the distillation of years of accomplishment that had imbued them with this magic, so he looked upon his friend with a new wonder of what those years had contained, the years between, since he parted from this man as a boy back on the old Pennsylvania farm; and that he looked upon a rare thing, a life rewarded.

XVI

THE COUNCIL was over, the council fire long since fallen to ashes, the people dispersed to their rest. The guests of the *casa* had lingered for a time in close discussion but had departed at last for their quarters, some of them shaking their heads doubtfully. It was not easy to forget at once the insult of outrage, as they thought; they resented fiercely the death of young Cermenos.

"But that was war," Andy had said reasonably. He refrained from pointing out that it was also disobedience of his orders.

Afterward Andy, and Carmel, and Djo, and Leslie, and Amata, and Braidwood had sat still later in the *sala,* for this was only reasonable that Carmel should hear. And first Andy would talk, and then Braidwood, Andy briefly and sketchily, as was his usual wont save on occasion, Braidwood with the polished ease and fluency of the experienced man of the world he was. Carmel listened, with occasional questions, occasional small exclamations of surprise or wonder. For, beginning with the day's doings and their conclusion in the council of the evening, it was necessary for their understanding to go on back and back into the past for explanation. Russell Braidwood must explain his presence and the potency of that presence, and that involved something of San Francisco, and his business there, and Jake Conger, and what was his business, and how it came about that Russell had influence with Jake; and that in turn led across seas and continents to a great commercial house, and Russell's rise in it, and his wanderings in its service, until the narrative thus returned again to San Francisco.

"I was at Monterey." He repeated what he had told Andy on the hill. "I heard vaguely of trouble in the valley. If there was trouble I knew my beloved nephew would be in it. So I rode up to see. That, señora, is how I happened to be here. Until I arrived, I had not the remotest idea that Andy was here." He looked quizzically at Leslie, who was somewhat flushed. "My nephew referred to his host only as Don Andreo. So I did not know until I had talked with you, señora, on my arrival. I feel flattered even now that you so instantly trusted me, señora. I might well have been a spy."

Andy looked at her keenly, for this point had been in the back of his mind. But Carmel was undisturbed. She laughed with a gentle and derisive scorn.

"I am not a fool, señor," said she. "I saw your face—when I told you my name." She added, "It was so happee," she explained to Andy. "You mus' be the great *amigo* in the old day."

"Yes." Braidwood was thoughtful. "And yet—it is queer." He turned to Andy. "Do you realize that we knew each other only a little over three weeks and saw each other just three times? And that was over thirty years ago! Señora, the first time we met we fought with each other over nothing until we both fell into muddy ice water, and the last time——"

"The las' time his *padrasto*, the bad man, he whip you, the horse, and order that you never come no more," supplied Carmel.

"You know all about it!" cried Braidwood.

Carmel nodded her small sleek head.

"*Sí,*" she assented. "I know all about heem. That was not easy, but I have live with heem nearly twenty years." She smiled her slow smile in Andy's direction. "It tak' twenty years," she added. Andy grinned at her.

"Well!" Braidwood considered this. "I never did go back to the farm—could go back," he amended, "not until five years later. I was away five years. Then I did. Strangers. Nobody knew anything. I never could find out." He looked toward Andy.

"I tried to kill the brute," he said simply. "Then I ran away. My grandmother died."

"He weel tell you"—Carmel answered Braidwood's look of expectation comfortably—"sometime. If you ask the many question mos' careful." She smiled at Andy affectionately, then at Braidwood with so complete a wisdom of understanding that he laughed.

"But through all these years," said he, "in spite of the fact that I never heard of him again, that I did not even know if he was alive or dead, I always thought of him, as you say, as a great friend—I think, in a way, as my greatest friend, though I have had a full life and have met a many."

"I think I shall love you for that, señor," said Carmel simply.

Andy shifted uncomfortably. A faint color showed beneath the bronze of his skin. Carmel uttered again her soft mischievous laugh.

"He think so too," said she, "but he cannot say. Never can he say."

"Shucks!" muttered Andy.

"You think this cur-ious, señor," said Carmel in her slow, painstaking way. "I do not find it so. Do you know our California? Have you watch how the groun' is hard like the iron, and it is brown and dry and bare like the estone? There come the leetle small rain, and it estop, and for a long, long time there is no more. The groun' he's just the same, brown and dry and bare. And then, after long, long time come more rain. And, pronto! In two-three-four hour the groun' is not bare but is all green. You have seen that, señor?"

"Yes," said Braidwood.

"That also is cur-ious, is it not? A magic? But it is not a magic. It is because in the heart of the earth"—she placed her hand on her bosom—"something is there that waits. Until the good God send the rain."

Braidwood looked at her with eyes in which was a new respect.

"Señora," said he, "you are very charming—and very wise!"

"*Gracias, señor,*" said Carmel.

2

It was well along toward morning. The others had long since gone to bed, but Andy and his new-found friend had lingered on, and lingered on, bringing together the ragged edges of the years to fit neatly into continuity. Now the dawn grayed the windows, and they were surprised.

"Too late for bed now," said Andy. "Let's go for a ride."

Braidwood assented and found himself laughing at himself. He had ridden most of the day before and had sat up all the night, and he had not the iron habitude of the old Mountain Man to such excursions. Yet he was willing, even eager, for the excursion, as for a refreshing bath in the morning.

"I don't know where my *mozo* has made off to," he told Andy. He laughed. "I don't even know where is my room, or my portmanteau, for that matter."

"We don't need him; we'll get our own hosses," said Andy.

Stampede 257

They stole out of doors and across the dimness to the corral, where the riding animals selected for the day threw up their heads and snorted at their appearance; and Andy, to Russell's admiration, roped two of them with seemingly careless flip casts, and they picked saddles at random from the pegs and so rode quietly away.

"We'll be back before anybody wants 'em," said Andy. "Besides, there's plenty of saddles."

"You've a lot of skills, haven't you, Andy?" observed Russell, half curiously, apropos of the accuracy of the roping. "Your life has taught you a good many of them. Do you remember our shooting match with the old rifle? And how you threw the knife at a mark on the stump? Can you still do that?"

"I couldn't do much with it then," said Andy. "I l'arned how later, on the plains."

Braidwood laughed amusedly.

"I thought you miraculous as you were then," said he; "I still do. I never learned many skills—I can ride a little, fence a little. That's about all. I've never carried a pistol because I never learned to shoot. It's safer."

Andy nodded agreement to this last.

"As for what you call skills," said he, "there ain't much to that. They're just what a man has use for in the way he lives. Tools, sort of. A man looks foolish lugging around a lot of tools he won't ever have use for. I reckon," said Andy shrewdly, "you've got a lot of tools I wouldn't even know the names of."

They let it go at that and rode on down the valley in sociable silence. They had talked much that night, and in face of the growing morning there was nothing to say.

The light strengthened. Far across the greater valley beyond the hills, the tops of the ranges were gilt with sun. Linnets, orioles, and vireos in the treetops were awakening to song. Below them the chirping birds were very busy, arguing officiously the dominance of day against the last reluctant yielding of night. The floor of the valley was milky blue with mists crouching below the triumphantly growing imminence of the sun.

"Kind of purty, isn't it?" said Andy.

Braidwood breathed deep, again and again, of the air's freshness, which of a sudden seemed to have grown perceptibly cooler. He remarked on this. Andy nodded.

"Always that way at dawn," said he. "Ef'n I was blind, I'd know the dawn by the taste of it."

Braidwood reined in his horse the better to look about him.

"Where does your land go?" he asked.

Andy laughed.

"She's supposed to begin over yander, beyond that low *puerto suelo*," said he, "but Leslie's been telling me nobody could even guess where she begins. I've sent for a surveyor to Monterey. But back of us she goes as far as you can see over the slopes, and a sight farther. She's a fine *rancho*."

"Let's ride over to the *puerto suelo* and see what it looks like at the boundaries. Is it good land? For farming, I mean."

"It's bottom land—and water. Why?"

"That's where you'll have your trouble, even if your title's right."

"That's what Leslie says. I reckon I better look after it."

"I reckon you'd better." Braidwood imitated him dryly.

They turned up the slope of the hill to the crest of the low ridge, along which they rode slowly in the direction of the *puerto suelo*. The valley of the *milpas* and the grainfields lay at their right. Shortly they came opposite the wagon encampment. It slept. Except for the lazy rise of a smoke spiral from a dying fire there was no motion at the camp proper. Scattered over the sidehill opposite, horses were preparing to abandon grazing for the luxury of the first sun warmth. Andy looked down speculatively.

"What you so tickled about?" asked Russell, struck by Andy's unmistakable pleasure.

"They got no guards—for themselves or hosses," said Andy.

For a moment Braidwood did not get this; then he understood his friend's gratification at this evidence he was trusted.

"Poor cusses," continued Andy. "They come a long way for land—a long way, and a hard way. Thought it lay free for the takin', all over the place. All they want is farms. It ain't right."

"But surely there's plenty of land!" cried Braidwood. "Good Lord, man, I never saw a rich country more thinly settled!"

"Not free land," amended Andy; "it's all been took up, one way or another. Except maybe over in the big Valley. That's a long ways. Oh yes, there's a plenty of land, and it's cheap. Why, you can get you some of the *pueblo* lands, over Soledad way, or maybe what's left of the mission lands for most nothing—two bits an acre, maybe. But," added Andy dryly, "you got to have the two bits. These folks ain't got a cent."

They rode on slowly. Suddenly Braidwood stopped

again, this time with a jerk that wrenched his horse's head around.

"What's that?" he asked sharply.

"What?" Andy's voice was unnaturally mild.

Braidwood pointed.

"There. In those trees. It looks like a man—hanging!"

Andy appeared to look.

"So it does," he agreed.

"Ransom!" cried Braidwood in a flash of illumination.

"Seems likely," Andy agreed again. "Didn't lose much time."

"You knew of this?" he accused.

"Seth did speak of it," Andy acknowledged. "Seemed, way he put it, a likely way to head off trouble. Sure to be trouble for somebody," he added. "It's the man's natur'. Seth asked my advice."

"You approved!" Braidwood was obviously shocked.

Andy looked at him with what Braidwood perceived to be a faint surprise.

"Why not?" he asked simply. "You find a rattlesnake, you stomp on him. You don't leave him loose to sink his fangs in you—or some other feller—next time you come along."

They rode on. Braidwood was no greenhorn. He had

gone through the Vigilance of 1851 in San Francisco. But even that experience had not quite prepared him for this tranquil attitude of indifference. He looked covertly askance at his friend. Andy met his glance.

"It ain't purty," he acknowledged. "I don't like hanging. I think myself I'd have shot him. Depends how a man's been brought up, I suppose. I sort of halfway expected I mout have to do it." He examined his friend's face keenly, again reined in his horse. "Look here, Russ," said he, "this man had it in for Djo—for Leslie, too, for that matter. And for you and for me and for these folks down yere. He's the killer kind, and, what I hear, he's trained with a rough lot. Sooner or later he's going to git somebody, and git him in the back. No two ways about it. There's no sense having to be always looking out for that sort of thing. No manner of sense. Nobody's going to protect you ef'n you don't protect yourself. I don't like it any better than you do. And, as I said, it ain't purty. No sense in that, either. They ought not to leave him hanging there. On our way back we'll just stop and speak to Seth Williams about it. Let's ride."

He apparently dismissed the subject from his thoughts. But Braidwood could not do so, at least for some time. He could acknowledge the good sense of Andy's point of view, but he could not yet understand it, nor appreciate that here also he was looking upon a darker distillation of the years between.

3

On the return journey toward the *casa* the two stopped again atop the ridge overlooking the small valley in which were encamped the settlers. Neither had spoken for some time. Each pursued his own train of thought. Both started to speak at the same instant. Each deferred to the other with a laugh.

"I was thinking of those folks down there," said Andy under Braidwood's insistence. "They ain't the bad sort at all. Ef'n the country's going to be settled, I'd ruther see that class come in than many others. They've been raised to take care of themselves. That kind makes purty good neighbors, ef'n you understand them."

Braidwood looked at him keenly.

"What you driving at, Andy?" he asked.

"Why, I just thought"—Andy looked embarrassed—"that a'ter all, they're Americans, and purty good Americans—and I got more'n fifty thousand acres here—all they want is just farms, where they can make a living——"

"I thought so," Braidwood interrupted with a laugh. "I've seen it coming."

"Wouldn't take more'n a couple thousand acres," said Andy.

Braidwood laid his hand affectionately on the other's arm.

"What you need, are going to need, in this new dispensation, is a business manager, Andy; and you'd better get one before you're stripped bare. The old days are gone, and they won't come back. The country is going to swarm with men out for what they can get, sharpers, and what are called legitimate businessmen. You won't be able to cope with them. They'll get everything you've got."

"I reckon I'll have something to say about that. I can keep what's mine!"

"You don't even know the words," said Braidwood bluntly. "Your rifle will do you no good. I've been talking to Leslie this afternoon. That boy is smart."

"He's going to make a fine man," agreed Andy gravely.

"From what he tells me your boundaries and your titles are in a mess, and if you don't straighten them out pretty soon you may find you have no title at all."

"You think there's something in that, then?" Andy looked troubled and for the first time somewhat impressed. "Well, I've sent to Monterey for a surveyor."

"That part's all right. And what will you do then?"

"I don't know," confessed Andy.

"Did you know this," demanded Braidwood, "that it is the law that every claimant—*every* claimant, mind you—of land under a Spanish or a Mexican grant must present his claim for endorsement with all documentary and other evidence within two years? And that failing this endorsement the land becomes part of the public domain? And that the two years are almost up?"

"No, I didn't," confessed Andy. "I've been too busy here at the *rancho*."

"Nor your neighbors either, I'll warrant."

"What do you do about it?" asked Andy with some anxiety, for the hearing of this from Braidwood impressed him.

"Present your proof to the Commissioners." Braidwood hesitated whether to go on. "And then, probably, appeal their decision to local courts, and after that to the Supreme Court." He laughed at Andy's expression. "It won't come to that. I'll engineer it for you. Jake Conger is under certain obligations to me."

"Jake Conger? The fellow you was telling us about?"

"A lawyer," said Braidwood briefly. "I'll attend to it."

Andy knit his straight brows.

"How about Ramon? Don José? Don Nicolas? All the others? They in the same fix?"

"I should think likely."

"Do you suppose you could—that this Conger could ——"

The horses stretched out their necks, dragging the reins through lax fingers. Having thus filched enough slack from their riders' inattention, they proceeded to crop mouthfuls of grass which they tried to masticate around the obstruction of their long spade bits. This was an intricate process, with little actual sustenance, but undoubtedly a pleasing taste. They stared abstractedly into the distance and revolved the soft cud over and over the rollers of the bits, and green saliva stained the silvered plates at the sides of their mouths.

Braidwood did not answer directly.

"Andy," said he, "I don't know the back country of your *rancho*, of course, but isn't there good farming land there?"

"Some. In pockets and spots. But that back there is mostly grazing land. The land good for farming is mostly down in the bottoms here, toward the river."

Braidwood nodded. "And," he pointed out, "I won't conceal from you that you'll find, when your survey is made, that you're likely to lose quite a strip of that. I don't know how much, but quite a lot. These old claims always take in a heap more than was actually granted."

"Think so?" said Andy. "Well, there's plenty."

"And," persisted Braidwood, "you're proposing—or hinting, anyway—that you give away a couple of thousand acres more, for that's what it amounts to. How much you going to have left?"

"Enough to raise what I need. I'm a cattleman, not a farmer," said Andy stoutly.

"The future is farming, not cattle," returned Braidwood succinctly. "What about Djo?"

Andy shifted uneasily in his saddle. The horse, recalled by the movement, stopped munching at the grass.

"You see?" said Braidwood. "'I can keep what's mine.'" He quoted Andy's words. "Can you? Will you?"

Andy brooded, his face dark.

"It's tough. They are good folks," he said at last. "I don't know what they're going to do!" He brightened with an idea. "This extra land you spoke of that mout be outside the survey. Quite a strip, you said. How about that? That's good farming land. Why can't they take that up? How much of it you reckon there'd be?"

"I couldn't say until the survey is made." Braidwood

answered the second question first. "But in any case they cannot have that."

"Why not?"

"Because," said Braidwood deliberately, "I intend to file on it myself."

"Oh!" said Andy. He touched his horse to set it in motion. The animal stretched its neck for one last mouthful of grass, snorted and leaped as the spur bit its flanks. But Andy's face was inscrutable. He instantly subdued his mount to a walk. Braidwood spurred alongside.

"If I straighten things out, surely I should get something out of it, shouldn't I?" said he.

"I reckon so," said Andy shortly. He looked straight ahead of him. Braidwood surveyed him for a moment in private amusement, but his own eyes were soft.

"Andy," said he, "stop your horse and listen to me. I'm going to tell you what I'm going to do. I've been thinking and figuring things over while we've been riding about."

"Go ahead." Andy reined in his horse.

"I'm going to take up, for myself, whatever of the present *rancho* the survey cuts out. And I'm not going to turn it over for settlement either to these Missourians or anybody else. I'm going to keep it as it is. That's the first thing I'm going to do.

"The second thing I'm going to do is this: I'm going to buy sufficient land of the Soledad *pueblo,* or the mission, to settle these people on farms to suit them."

For the first time Andy looked at his friend.

"Anon?" he inquired in blank astonishment. Braidwood repeated. "What for?" asked Andy.

"To head you off from giving them your good bottom land, you old fool," returned Braidwood crisply, "for that's exactly what you'd do. These may be good people, as you say, but you don't want them too close to you. They'd kill your game all off, for one thing, and," added Braidwood dryly, "for all you say, I'd prefer to have them live out of walking distance if I was going to raise chickens."

Andy burst out laughing. In the notes of his laughter was an exaggeration that, to Braidwood's keen ear, measured a secret relief and perhaps as secret an apology.

"I'm afraid you're right on that, Russ," said he. "It's a first-class idee. I'll do it."

"You will not," Braidwood negatived flatly. "I thought of it first, and I'm going to do it myself."

"But why should you?" Andy was puzzled again. "These folks ain't nothing to you."

"Not one thing," agreed Braidwood cheerfully.

"And a'ter all, it's my *rancho* they're kept off from."

"That's just the point," said Braidwood, smiling.

Andy shrugged his shoulders in despair.

"I s'pose it's going without sleep," said he, "or else mebbe I'm getting old and my mind is wore out. Or else I'm crazy. Or else you are."

"None of 'em," said Braidwood promptly. "I told you you ought to have a business manager, and I'm trying to fix it to get you one. No, this is serious. I'll quit fooling. But first answer me one thing, and answer me fairly and honestly. I know you will, for I mean it. Do you like my nephew Leslie?"

He felt Andy's direct look boring into him.

"I come to love him like a son—we all do," Andy finally answered with sober directness.

"Would you feel like keeping him on at the *rancho?* I don't mean for a visit, but for always, to learn ranching, grow up with it."

"By the 'tarnal!" Andy's face lighted up. "Would you want him to do that? Why, he and Djo———"

"All right," Braidwood cut him short. "Then here is my proposal to you. I shall, as I said, take up whatever surplus land the survey shows to exist. That I shall turn back to you. This *rancho* should be kept intact."

"Look here," cried Andy, relapsing in his heat to the vernacular, "I don't need no pay to——"

"Shut up," commanded Braidwood, "and listen to me! I'm not offering to pay you anything, and I'm not offering to give you anything, either. Wait till I get through talking and then see what you have to say. Do you always go off half cock like this?"

"Go ahead," said Andy, made meek by his own favorite figure of speech.

"In addition," went on Braidwood in dry business tones, "I shall permit you to reimburse me for the moneys I expend in getting your friends their farms. They are your friends," he pointed out, "not mine. You shall reimburse me for that—and also for whatever lands I take up and turn back into the *rancho*—by an interest, an undivided interest, in the *rancho* itself, the amount of that interest to be proportional, by appraisement." He watched Andy's groping comprehension with delighted amusement. "In other words," he explained, "I'm trying to buy in, in a small way, as your partner. If it's agreeable to you," he added.

Andy uttered a wild Indian yell that startled not only both horses, but Braidwood himself. The latter dodged a mighty swing that probably would have dislodged him from his saddle.

"My pardner!" shouted Andy. "Why, you damned old horny toad! Ef'n it's agreeable to me!" he mocked. "You mis'able hound! Hell's flames! By the 'tarnal, I could chase my tail around like a dawg! Is *that* what you're driving at? To blazes with all that monkey work! That ain't necessary, and you ought to know it. I'll *give* it to you, and gladly! You're my pardner right this minute, from now on. You fix it up. Sooner the better. I'll make you over a half share, and we'll run the thing together—you and me. Braidwood & Burnett, Business Manager and Field Boss!"

In his delight the grave hard lines of Andy's face had softened, so that Braidwood stared at it with amazement and a little awe, for he thought to see again the boy he had known so many years ago.

4

"Well," yielded Andy in reluctant resignation, after the ensuing discussion, "ef'n you won't, you won't! But I sort of halfway hoped you'd be here with us, at Folded Hills, and that——"

"Don't forget that I've a great deal of business of my own. You'll be seeing more of me than you want," Braidwood interrupted. "I like this. It is California. The city is not. I'll be here a lot. Though the city is an interesting place, at that. You'll have to come to see me there. No, Andy; all I want is enough share in the place to have some say-so when you try to give it all away."

"Your say-so would always be good anyhow," Andy assured him earnestly, "and glad to get it."

"I know. But then too, in case of any legal trouble I'd have some legal standing, so I could do something. And then there's the matter of Leslie. It makes a great difference to a boy of that age whether he has a real stake in what he's doing, no matter how small it is."

"I reckon you're right," agreed Andy, but still with reluctance. A passing thought creased his brown skin with sly wrinkles. "I expect that someday Djo and Amata will each git equal shares of what I've got, so Leslie mout git to be a half owner after all."

Braidwood looked at him sharply.

"Nothing could be better," he agreed, "but they're children! She can't be more than twelve or thirteen."

"Twelve," said Andy. "I'm not talkin' about now. Near as I can make out, they got about as much use for each other as Benito has for grasshoppers. I can't see any symptoms at all. But Carmel——" He stopped, laughed deprecatingly.

"Your wife's opinions have my profoundest respect," said Braidwood.

"Carmel says it's a nat'ral ef'n Leslie stops here long enough."

"I sincerely hope she's right," said Braidwood heartily. "I'd like nothing better for him, myself. But," he warned, "be mighty careful! The surest way to spoil the whole business is to show in any way that you want it to happen!"

"That's what Carmel says." Andy hesitated. "Now about Ramon, and Don José, and Don Nicolas—and I'm not so sartin Don Sylvestro——"

Braidwood threw up both arms with a laugh.

"Hold on! Hold on!" he cried. "You're overestimating my influence. I can't take on the whole of California."

"I'm not asking you to," returned Andy, "just these. They're my neighbors—have been for nigh twenty year: some of 'em are *parientes*."

"Give me a list," said Braidwood. "I'll do what I can."

"Come on," urged Andy. "Let's get back to the folks!"

He struck spurs to his chestnut. They raced away in the headlong California fashion, full speed, helter-skelter, without slackening pace for hill slopes or roughness of ground. Andy's eagerness grew. He must get home to carry to all his world his satisfactions.

5

Djo marveled aloud at the way things work out in this strange world.

"Think," said he to Leslie, "if you just hadn't happened along!"

He seemed to consider, in the extravagance of his delight in the arrangement and his friendship, that the outcome was all due to Leslie, as, indeed, in a way it was. But Amata was not impressed.

"Humph!" she sniffed. "I can't see he's done anything—except to pick out a good uncle!"